Ellen

Ellen

Tom Rudloff

ELLEN

Printed in the United States of America.

ISBN 978-1-949746-44-0 (Paperback)
ISBN 978-1-949746-45-7 (Digital)

Lettra Press books may be ordered through booksellers or by contacting:
Lettra Press LLC
18229 E 52nd Ave.
Denver City, CO 80249
1 303 586 1431 | info@lettrapress.com
www.lettrapress.com

1

The strawberry blond little girl wipes the breeze-blown hair from her eyes. Ellen is under the shade tree in her front yard. The summer day is hot, but beautiful. At 6 she's not really thinking about the heat or the beauty of the day as much as her pretend life with her babies and their daddy. Ellen lives in a neighborhood near the city. Their house is not the nicest, but the love makes it a home. She feels safe to be outside by herself and raises her pretend family in the same loving way her Mommy raises her. She works hard at preparing the imaginary supper and still taking care of her baby dolls and cleaning the rooms of her house that lie within walls of her mind. It's a fairy tale life that is oh, so busy. Though she rushes around and hurries like her own mommy, the pressure is pretend and the emergency is held at bay by her imagination.

"Now I better stir that soup one more time. Johnny you play nice with your baby sister. She's little, and you have to be careful with babies." She rushes over to a rock she has set on a board that is her phone. "Hello? Yes dear, we are having a good day. I'll have supper for you when you get home from work. Good bye, love you." She hangs up her rock and goes back to her cooking.

This is playing and having fun. Having constant conversation not only with her dolls, but also with imaginary friends, and the one she calls the daddy. Life, as she sees it, is good, as it should be at 6. Most of the problems that come up during this pretend time are the challenges that she has heard her Mommy face. Though Ellen doesn't understand the issues or the solutions, she faces them with the same resolve that

Mommy does, and everything always works out. The Mom can take care of it. That's what Mommy always tells her, 'everything will be ok'; so that is what she believes and tells her own pretend family.

Her mommy is pretty and nice, always giving her a smile and love. She seems happy while she is busy and working hard. It is strange to her, though, Mommy also seems bothered. Looking and watching, she would sometimes sing with the radio and dance with Ellen in the kitchen. It's fun with Mommy, but only when Daddy isn't home. She loves her Daddy, but Mommy is so different when he is around. She doesn't see her pretty smile as much, nor is there any singing. Often, when Ellen goes to bed, they will yell at each other; and she can hear her mommy cry. Most of the time it's when Mommy asks for money for food or shoes or to pay the bills. Daddy often yells at her for wasting so much and always asking for more.

So when her play turns to interaction with the daddy, the conversation is a little bit more stern and louder. It isn't the sweet, loving voice that you hear when she talks with her babies. This person, the daddy, never helps, is around, or understands. She has to take care of the babies herself, and she can and does. She knows that 'she doesn't need him', and 'he can just leave'. 'She will do it, but she does need money for grocery shopping.' The play is just that, play; and is so much fun she looks forward to each day of playing house. The babies always get better when they are sick, things always work out her way, all her answers are the right ones, and the daddy never makes her cry. She just loves being a mommy and always watches what her Mommy does so she can do it the same way. Shopping, driving the car, putting on makeup, these everyday things add to Ellen's fantasy world of playing house.

Sometimes she plays that the daddy is her hero. He keeps her safe and protected, just like the knights that her mommy tells her about. Sometimes at night her mommy tells her stories before bed time. Often they are about brave men that save ladies in danger. They always live happily ever after. All the princes in all the movies she watches are very nice and try hard to make the princess happy and take care of them. They are tough against the bad guys, talking to them in a mean way to make the bad guys scared of them, but when they talk to the princess they are always soft and kind. You can see that the princes try really hard to do the right thing and help the princess. Sometimes things hurt them, but they never stop. The heroes never fail to grit their teeth, and sometimes even sweat to do whatever needs to be done to save the princess. At the end the princess and the prince are so happy to be together. Her mommy says "and they lived happily ever after". Ellen knows that it's like that for everyone, and that's the way she plays house.

Her real Daddy is just like this. When he comes home he greets her with a big smile and picks her up and hugs her. Sometimes he will play with her and make her laugh. At times they sit on the couch and talk. Daddy asks her what she has been doing and tickles her and makes her giggle. He loves when she colors pictures for him and always wants her to give him kisses. At night he always says good night and calls her princess. Ellen always feels safe around her Daddy. When he is home, he sometimes takes her and her Mommy out to the store. She gets to hold his hand, and he talks to her when he's not too busy or looking at something. She loves her Daddy. He's a great guy and has told her he will keep getting her what she needs. He's so nice. She just wishes she could see him more. Often days and days go by and he's not at home. Mommy says he's working, but Ellen just wants him home. Maybe Mommy does, too. Ellen can remember when Daddy used to go to church with her and Mommy. Sunday was her favorite day. She loves going to church, and when Daddy was with them they were a whole family. She still goes to church with Mommy all the time, and she still loves the people and going, but it's not the same without Daddy.

Her Daddy does sometimes yell at her. She doesn't always know what he wants, and that makes him really mad. Other times he talks funny and walks like he's going to fall down. It's kind of scary. She cries and runs to her Mom, but that usually makes him madder. She is beginning to realize that it's easier when it's just her and Mommy. Daddy is the hero, and he is big and strong. Nothing bad can happen when Daddy is around. Mommy even tells her how much her Daddy loves her. It's just kind of hard for her to understand why she wants him home with them but is glad when he leaves.

At the end of the summer she gets to go to school. She has always been at home with Mommy and helps her do the shopping, clean the house, and cook. But now it is time for her to be a big girl and go to school. She will ride the bus and sit in a desk. She will have a teacher and make new friends. It all sounds so exciting, but who will be Mommy's helper, and what will it be like to be away from Mommy all day?

One evening Ellen and Mommy set off to go to the school to walk around and meet her teacher. Daddy was supposed to go with them, but Daddies are very busy. They waited for him, but Mommy said it would be ok, they would just go on by themselves, and tell Daddy all about it. When they walked in, they were greeted by some very nice people who gave them directions, a name tag, and some papers. Ellen got to sit on a bus and walk down the hall to the cafeteria. The best part was meeting her teacher. She seemed so nice and looked like a princess. Her hair was pretty, and her smile was so friendly. The teacher, somehow, already knew Ellen's name, and had picked out a desk especially for her. She and Mommy looked through the books that she would be using, and Ellen was even able to pet the gerbil in the cage. The teacher made school sound like so much fun that it made Ellen want to start very soon, but she wanted to make sure Mommy wouldn't be lonely.

When the teacher was talking to someone else, Ellen turned to Mommy and said, "If I go to school will you come with me?"

Mommy smiled and said that she had already gone to school, so she would just wait for her at home.

"But Mommy will you be scared by yourself? Who will be your helper?"

Mommy explained to her that it would be hard with no helper but she would do it, so Ellen could have fun and go to school and learn new things. Ellen was worried. She began to get scared and tell her Mommy she didn't want to go to school. They talked all the way home. Her Mommy said that when she was a little girl, she went to school and liked it. Mommy went on to tell her that she would be fine at home while Ellen was gone and would always be there when she came home. Mommy knew how to make Ellen feel better. She understood how Ellen felt and kept telling her everything would be ok. Ellen began to see what Mommy was telling her and felt much better that Mommy would be ok at home. Ellen now really wanted to go to school, but not if it would make Mommy sad. She didn't want Mommy to cry, but Mommy assured her she would be fine.

The day finally came. Ellen and Mommy were standing at the bus stop. Ellen didn't mind that everyone had new clothes and backpacks. Mommy had washed her clothes really clean and fixed her hair so very pretty. Daddy had told them both that he would give them money to buy school things, but now he said new stuff wasn't important to go to school. He had given her a big hug and made her laugh by tickling her until she screamed. Then he put her down and left. Mommy was sad, but Ellen said it was ok. That's when Mommy told her how she would make her clothes look like new and fix her hair, so it would be very pretty. Mommy was good at hair. She was pretty, and could make Ellen pretty. They found ribbons to match the dress that Mommy ironed. They even put ribbons around her shoelaces. Ellen was excited and ran to get on the bus when it pulled up. She got into her seat and sat next to the window. There was Mommy waving to her. She waved back until the bus pulled away. It was all so very exciting.

The ride wasn't very long, and she was able to find her classroom easily. When she walked into the room, she waved to her teacher. The teacher smiled a big, happy smile like she was glad to see her, just adding to Ellen's excitement. Some kids were crying, but Ellen ran straight to the desk the teacher had showed her that first night. It was on the outside row next to the windows. Seated in the desk next to hers was a little boy, his name was Ray. He looked at her and said hi. She replied and thought he must be nice. There was a little girl that walked by her and sat in the desk right behind her. Ellen turned around and said hi. They shared their names with each other and giggled. Why? They didn't know, but they were already friends. The teacher started the class, and Ellen turned around.

At recess, Ellen and her new best friend Beth ran around and played together. Often the other little girls joined in. Beth always had good games and fun ideas. Ellen thought it was neat to be her special friend. She was very hungry when lunch time came around. Mommy had packed her a lunch and she couldn't wait to eat it. She and Beth sat together and giggled in between each bite. Out on the playground, she never had so much fun; and the time went by quickly. Beth and Ellen sat together on the bus on the way home, talking, laughing, and sharing secrets. They made plans to sit together the next morning. Ellen's stop was first, and when she got to the front of the bus, she turned back and waved to Beth, then she went down the steps. Once off the bus, she ran to her Mom, bubbling over with excitement, talking 100 mph, to tell her everything that happened the entire day all in one sentence. Mommy was interested in every detail and had a million questions. Ellen looked forward to telling Daddy, too; but Daddy wasn't home.

The days clicked by. School came easily. She already knew her letters and could write them. That was just one of the things Mommy had taught her. Even adding was pretty cool, and Ellen enjoyed doing it. One of the funny things was the others in her classroom. Her teacher did turn out to be a princess. She was always nice and talked to her with kindness. The way she would help you to learn new things reminded Ellen of Mommy. Her teacher would even giggle at some things that she would say, just like Mommy did. She made school fun with songs and decorations on the walls, even dancing to music when it was too rainy to play outside. The other girls in the classroom seemed to be much like herself. They all enjoyed playing and laughing. Sometimes when she, Beth, and her other friends would be outside they would laugh until their stomachs hurt. They would play tag and swing, and have fun. The ones that made school strange was the boys. Out on the playground they would only play with the girls if a teacher would make up the game. If everyone had to make a circle, the boys never wanted to hold the girls' hands or even stand by them. It was weird. If they did play a game together, the boys always made fun of the girls and told them they weren't very good at the game. They sometimes made fun of each other and hurt each other's feelings. Then she and Beth started acting like they felt the same way about them. Boys were gross and had cooties. They never wanted to be around them and tried never to touch them. If somehow it did happen that they touched one of the boys, they had to use 'cootie spray' to get it off. Playing this way made Ellen feel silly. She really didn't like it, because Mommy had taught her to be nice to everyone. But she went along with it. Ellen didn't think about it much, but the boy that sat next to her, Ray, always seemed to be nice. He was different. When the other boys were around he would do as they did and stay away from the girls, but at their desks he was polite and nice to talk to. He even shared his crayons, because he had a 24 pack.

Something else very big happened this first year of school. Ellen realized that she needed Jesus. She knew she wanted God to forgive her for the times that she lied and disobeyed her parents. If she followed Jesus, she knew He would help her in school and at home. She felt bad about the times when she had done wrong things and wanted to tell God she was sorry and be forgiven. She always felt better when she had told Mommy or Beth she was sorry, and she now knew she wanted to do the same thing with God. Once her choice was made, she felt more secure and better about herself. She enjoyed church, school and other things even more. Now her Mom would talk to her about more important things like; how God would help her to make good choices and guide her to follow His plan for her life. God would make her life better, as she followed Jesus. One of the things that really interested her was that God had a plan for her life. Ellen asked about this the most. Her mother did her best to answer her questions without painting a pie in the sky, everything will be perfect picture. She did share that if Ellen would take God's Word as Truth and use it to direct her life as she grew up, she would have more answers and fewer questions. She went on to explain that God loved her and knew what was best for her. Mommy made sure to explain that sometimes life isn't easy.

"Oh, like trying to open the jelly jar lid that is stuck." Mommy giggled and agreed; but added that other things, too, can make life hard. Mommy went on to tell Ellen that God doesn't make all the hard things go away, like the stuck jelly jar lid, but helps us through them. Ellen listened and decided to believe what her Mommy had said.

Days, months, and years just flew by. In a child's mind, there is never any thought to where they were going. It was always "what is coming next." The people in her neighborhood never seemed to change. The people that were old were always old, the people that were young seemed to stay the same, and she noted no difference. Those who were nice, which most were, always waved or said hello. Some of those people always seemed happy. There was one couple in particular, the Bars. They were people that always seemed to smile. They would wave and talk to her if she stopped or came over. Sometimes she would ask Mommy if she could go over and visit with the Bars. Mommy would say 'if they are outside, and don't mind you talking'. They never did. They always welcomed her visits with smiles and bright eyes, and smiled wider when Ellen asked if it was ok if she talked to them. They would ask how she and her Mommy were doing, tell her what they were doing outside, even wanted to hear about school and her friends. They, like her teacher, and Mommy would giggle sometimes at the stories she would tell, but they always made her feel special. They never really had too much to say so Ellen would fill in the conversation. It was obvious that Mr. and Mrs. Bar really liked one another. They would talk to each other and poke fun. They often touched or pushed each other in fun and would laugh. They did things together; work or play. Mr. Bar seemed to be home a lot more often than her Daddy, and you could tell he wanted to be there. Even when they didn't agree, they seemed to just talk and not get mad and yell. That's not the way things worked at home. Ellen liked to be around the Bars. It made her feel different some how, special, and good.

2

Time and life was logged and moved by grades, first grade, second grade, then third grade, now fourth. She never marked the change in herself or in Mommy but, as she grew she began to note some of the differences in others. Not just old and young but also the differences in boys and girls, even men and woman, how they acted and reacted to different things and each other. Moms and Dads were not all the same either. The Bars next door and her friend Beth's parents. Each were unique. Some seemed to be good, some not so good. Some even seemed hard and painful. Ellen outgrew "Once upon a time," and "Happily ever after," but still, in most of the books she read, it talked about the Dad being a good person who was around and added good things into the home and family. Her favorite movie showed struggles and hard times that came upon a family but it also showed how the Dad continued to encourage and guide the family to work together and everything worked out. That movie showed a Mom and Dad that worked together and enjoyed being together even facing challenges and difficult times. She loved that movie, watching it over and over. She was beginning to see that Hollywood's picture may be what everyone wants, but it isn't what everyone gets. Nothing showed her this more than her own home.

Now that she was more aware, what she saw didn't always make her feel good. Her Mom didn't seem to be so nervous when her Dad was not around. But it was also clear that she didn't like it when he was gone. Though Ellen didn't understand what her Dad did when he was gone, she did catch on that he wasn't always working. Actually it became clear that he didn't have a regular job like other Daddy's did. Her Mom tried to hide it and make things as nice as possible, but Ellen was now very much aware that her family had a hard time just paying the bills and having food to eat. Their house wasn't the nicest on the street, but it was her home. Their car didn't always run but they managed. Other things became real to her also, if her parents had just started arguing if front of her recently, they learned very quickly how to do it well. There was no more waiting for Ellen to go to bed, it was more and more often. Or it might have been she just began to understand what was going on and couldn't ignore it.

Ellen couldn't help but want to understand. She would ask her Mom about these things, Dad and the way he was. Mom was always kind and patient, doing her best not to talk poorly about Ellen's father, but she was not going to lie. Most times when she was talking, her Mom would have tears rolling down her cheeks. Ellen didn't want to hurt her Mom, but she had all these questions, and in reality her Mom didn't seem to be hurt by the questions, it was that she was just hurt. It wasn't the questions; it was the life. It made Ellen sad to think that her Mom was so disappointed in the way her life had turned out. That things, whatever that included, didn't seem to work out the way she thought it would. Dad changed. By what her Mom told her, he was so cool when they met. He was always so polite and kind. As they dated and their relationship grew she knew she loved him. He was thoughtful and would call just to talk. He would go out of his way to see her and make her feel special. They could talk about anything; share dreams, and plans, always using the words we and us. But something had happened, he was different, in what he did and what he didn't do. Most of all it was easy to see that Daddy didn't like the change either. He was so very unhappy and didn't want anybody around him happy either. He kept trying to find something to make him happy but nothing ever seemed to work for him. By the way Ellen now saw it, the man of her mom's dreams had actually turned into a nightmare.

Ellen could clearly see the problems, but had not experienced much of what her mother talked about, until one day when Daddy came home after drinking more than usual and was meaner than most days. She was sitting in the living room having a snack after school when he walked in. The comments that he made were so hurtful. The way he thought was so strange. Telling her that she better not get fat, because men didn't like that. At 10 she never even thought about getting fat, much less what men might like or not like. Truth be known she was still fighting to keep her jeans up. Even when Ellen's tears of confusion flowed down her face, he didn't stop. He just got madder. What was left of their very strange relationship was being torn away. He kept going saying thoughtless hurtful things. Mommy came into the room and was just as stunned as Ellen was. Mommy yelled at Daddy not to talk so mean to her. She loved her Daddy and wanted to love him. Ellen didn't understand, she just backed out the front door with him still yelling at her. She was so very confused, what just happened. Most of what he said she didn't even understand, but it was obvious Daddy didn't think much of her and seemed not to have much hope that she would ever amount to anything. It was strange, confusing, and painful. He had never talked to her like that. She had never seen him like that. What had she done to change what he thought of her? What did she do to make him so mad at her? It was almost like it wasn't her Daddy. Like this was a different man. She never looked at him the same way again.

Later, after walking around the neighborhood a while, she saw that his car was once again gone. She went back into the house. Mom looked at her when she came through the door. Mom always knew how to help. Tears came to both their eyes, and Mom moved forward and hugged her. They both hung on to one another and cried. Yes, Mom reassured her that what he had said was not true, but the words had cut so deep it was hard to feel relief. They went to the living room and sat down. They talked for several hours about what had happened and the possible reasons as to why it happened and how neither one of them understood what prompted the outburst or the thought behind it. One thing that Mom was very clear about was it wasn't Ellen's fault, she did nothing wrong to provoke such an attack. Ellen's Mom was careful not to sound condemning, he was her Daddy and should be respected. Actually she guided Ellen to love her Daddy for the good in him and hate the drinking that always lit the fuse that caused him to explode. They committed to one another to pray for Daddy and not to give up on him. Then her Mom started talking about things she loved about Ellen's Dad. It brought to mind many good memories that Ellen had and they talked and laughed about the many different past experiences that they all three enjoyed.

School became a big part of Ellen's life. She could do well, but she had to keep the books open and pay attention in class. The reward came when her grades reflected her hard work. Learning didn't always come easily, but she did like figuring things out and understanding them. One day at school she heard that they had volleyball tryouts. She had played in PE class and liked it. Her Mom encouraged her to try out. Practices would be right after school, and they lived close enough that Ellen could walk home. The school volleyball coach was a man, and he was loud and hard. Truth be known Ellen and most of the girls were scared of him. The girls had to start attending practices, and he would cut the girls he didn't like. At least that's the way it looked to Ellen. The first night she was nothing short of nervous. The whistle was always blowing, orders were being barked out with great volume, and even reprimands if you didn't do it right. She just kept her head down and did what he said. She didn't even like to look at him and it was even scarier when he was looking at her. It took everything she had to go back the next day. After that she was hooked. Coach would push her and the others so hard they would sweat and puff like a train engines, but it fed some kind of fire inside her and she came to love it. The different things that he taught them about the game and how to play, made it so much fun and connected them together as a team. He was a different kind of person. He could yell out orders and even seem to get mad, but you always knew he was trying to help you to do better. Somehow you knew that what he was doing was good for you and the team. There was some kind of a bond here that Ellen had never experienced. He was her coach, nothing more, but if he would had barked, 'run through that fire,' she would have done it knowing that it was ok. The pain that she often felt before and the day after practice became part of that bond. It made her better. Ellen loved how he could push her to do things that she thought she couldn't.

When any of the girls did good he would yell, "That's it, that's it, good job!"

It made her smile whether he was talking to her or not. He was a great guy, and seemed to work as hard as they did, often running, jumping and participating in what he demanded of them. The team did ok, but coach always made you feel like a winner if you tried hard, and he could always tell the difference. Being a part of a team and being pushed really encouraged her. She would have jumped for the moon if coach would have asked her to. She just somehow knew that he would never have asked her to do anything that wasn't good for her or anything he didn't believe that she could do. He was special to her. This experience rolled over into other areas of her life. She pushed herself harder in her school work and even the chores around the house. This coach changed the way she looked at things. Maybe the way she looked at everything. Now she thought she could or at least she could try.

There was a game that Coach had built up real big. It was against a school that always beat his team. He kept telling them that this year would be different. This year they could do it. He pushed them harder than usual, and all the girls responded by giving all they had, all a 10 year old girl could give. The day of the game the score continued to go back and forth, neither team had it easy. The floor was wet with their sweat and the air filled with their desire to win. The whole crowd could feel it, often on their feet cheering them on. They were playing like professionals; not with that kind of skill, because at 10 they couldn't, but with that kind of effort and determination. Both teams listened to their coaches and made the plays and adjustments that they directed. Volleys seemed to last forever. The fight was fought with no thought of backing down. The coaches never sat down but breathed life and strength into their teams with each step they paced and every order barked. At the final point of the set, Ellen's team was behind and the match was lost. She was so disappointed and then so surprised. Both coaches brought their teams out onto the gym floor together and were praising all the players for the game. They were patting the girls on the back and commenting on the plays made. Both of these men wanted to win that match and would have fought to the very end to do it, yet now they laughed and joked, congratulating each other and each other's players as well. It was like there was no winner or loser. These men loved the game and stood in awe of the heart each girl showed out on the floor. That made such a statement to Ellen. Her effort did matter and measure up. Her coach showed her something about herself that she liked. You're a winner if you heartily apply yourself, if you give all you have, if you give of yourself. That's a winner.

In the car her Mom couldn't stop talking about the game and how they all played. Her Mom had given a ride to some of the other girls on the team. As they dropped each them off there was a short but very loud celebration. So strange, they had lost the game, but there was a clear victory here. When they were alone in the car, Ellen's Mom asked her to talk to God about what she was experiencing now. Her Mom went on to explain that God was really showing her some amazing things, and she should ask Him to help her learn what He was wanting her to know. Mom went on to explain what she was talking about. How God was letting her see victory in loss and even more important how God was giving her friendships and relationships in her life that would be a blessing in the future. Ellen tried to understand. She was only 10; but she did what Mom had asked, and talked to God about it; though her young mind really didn't know what to say, it seemed like a good idea and wanted God in her life. Afterwards she did feel she could better see the blessings of her teammates, her Mom, and her coach.

School also brought more friends. The girls in her class really liked being together. They would talk and giggle and laugh at the silliest things. It was so much fun. Some of them would make plans and meet after school or on Saturdays. They would do each other's hair and talk, or play games and talk, or walk in the park and talk. It was so cool. Ellen grew up as an only child but now she and Beth became like sisters, even though Beth chose not to play volleyball, their relationship grew. Ellen called Beth's Mom and Dad, Mom and Dad, as did Beth to her Mom. They loved it when others were with them but the two of them were nearly inseparable. There was something special here and they both knew it.

Ellen spent many nights over at Beth's house. They would talk and play games, watch TV shows, and listen to music. She quickly noticed the difference in Beth's Dad and how he acted with Beth's Mom and interacted with her and Beth. He reminded her of Mr. Bar, the neighbor. These men were funny and didn't make you feel uncomfortable or uneasy. There was such a difference in the way people were and how they treated others. At times she felt sorry for those who always seemed to be mad or mean and who treated others poorly, almost, so it seemed to her, so no one would like them. That was the way she saw her Dad. Always doing things that would keep hurting himself. Now Beth's Mom was so much like hers. They were both fun to be around and kind to both the girls. They would talk to Ellen and Beth like one of the girls, asking questions and being interested in what they were interested in. The Moms had become friends themselves, which just added to the very special relationship that Ellen and Beth had. It was so cool when all 5 of them would go to one of Ellen's volleyball games or to ice cream after wards. They all had a great time like they were all family. As time went by each of them felt close to the other.

She and Beth would play dress up and liked playing house. They had their favorite dolls and they would be the Moms. Ellen would always have a family like others that she knew. She would act like her Mom, doing the activities that she watched her doing, but the Dad was always like someone else. Without giving it much thought, the life she lived while playing house, was not the home she lived in. Her desires were for something other than that. She would pretend that her husband was fun and funny yet helpful and always came home for dinner unless of course that he had to work late. He was a hard worker and worked hard for the family. The girls would have tea and act like they were real ladies with good manners and respectable. This is the way they saw different women that were around; their own Moms, teachers, ladies at church. Their dream world was wonderful and fun. Yes at times there were the tears. Challenges and pain exist no matter what age you are. Life indeed is hard when you are older or 10 years old. When things like this happened family and friends help you through it. Beth, her parents, and of course Mom, were always there to help dry a tear and shed a few of their own with her.

3

It was sad to see but the relationship between Mom and Dad continued to melt away. When Dad was home, Ellen tried to stay out of the way. Their interaction was only somewhat good when he was drunk and wanted to talk to his 'little girl'. That's the way it was. If he didn't ignore her, he cut her down; or he was drunk and wanted to talk about silly stuff. She missed the idea of the Daddy of years ago. The one who she would run to and jump in his arms when he walked through the door. She could feel his hugs and remember giggling when he tickled her. She longed for the knight in shining armor, her hero. Now she knew he only did those things after he had been drinking and now when he wasn't he often had no time for her. She longed for his attention so much that even when he was drunk, she would talk to him so that they could be together, but it always made her lonely. She wanted his approval. She knew he wasn't perfect, she wasn't looking for perfect. In her mind the armor could have rust and dents, that would be ok. Ellen wanted him to notice that she was growing up, that she was doing well in school. She wanted him to know Beth and like her. There was a great longing for him to be her Dad and they would be a family. Growing up made her see him for who he was, and she didn't like it. That in turn made her sad and feel bad that she felt that way about him.

What bothered her as well was what it did to Mom. At times it drained her of the vibrant person that she was. The shine in her eyes and the fun, mischievous smile was seen less and less whenever he was home. As the years passed, Ellen wondered what would become of them. There was so little left of the relationship. Dad came and went, and that set the ebb and flow of the home's attitude. Mom did her best to make it a good place, a nice home for her and Ellen; but a person can only control their own actions, not the actions of others. Mom put a lot of effort into enjoying the life she and Ellen had, but that can't replace the relationship between a husband and a wife. Ellen wanted her Mom to be happy, and for the most part she seemed to be. There was still something that she longed for and missed.

Eleven turned into twelve, which turned into thirteen, and eighth grade made her more aware of the others around her and how they felt. As happy as her Mom often was, Ellen still knew she was lonely, and what Ellen saw concerned her. Mom started noticing other men, and it was obvious that she wanted them to notice her too. She would look at them in a different way and say things that encouraged men to talk more to her. Ellen's mom was very pretty. She didn't need help drawing attention to herself, but that was what she was doing. Her skirts kept getting higher, and her shirts were tighter. Ellen didn't like the way this made her Mom look. Oh she was pretty and cute, but this stole from her the beautiful women that she was. She lost being special and beautiful and gained only glares and sultry looks. Even the boys in her class would say things about how her Mom looked, but she never took it as if they were complimenting her, it was embarrassing. The tone of their voice made Ellen mad and hurt. Ellen knew her Mom was not like that. She tried to explain her feelings to her Mom, telling her what she saw and heard, and changes would be made for a week or so, then it was back to the tight and tiny. The longer looks with her head tilted just a little sent signals to the men around her that she was interested in them. She would laugh and open her eyes wide, and they would move a little closer to her. Ellen understood. Her Mom felt the same way she did. They both were looking for a closer relationship with the important man in their life, Mom with her husband, Ellen with her Dad. Mom was just struggling with poor choices to satisfy this need in her. At Ellen's age she didn't know what to think about all of this. This wasn't who her Mom was, so who is she now.

Ellen's Mom had no one to talk to. She loved her husband, or the man he was. It just tore her up inside when he would come home. He was so close and yet so far away. Everything she needed and nothing that she wanted. Then it would tear her up when he left again. It was hard to put it together. She longed to see that smile on his face that told her that he loved her. The twinkle in his eye when he would kid her. The bump or nudge. All these were the confirming actions of love of the man she longed for. She understood that things and people change but this was too much. Her husband should be by her side, not here today gone tomorrow. He should have care and concern for her and Ellen. His words and actions spoke volumes. He no longer held anything back, there was no filter. He never gave reasons, just that his life was all about him and Ellen and her Mom were nothing more than a burden. She needed love, acceptance, a close relationship, someone.

Ellen found, too, that the attention she was beginning to get from the boys at school made her feel good. They would stop and talk to her and make her laugh. She started being more concerned about what she wore, she would make sure her hair was right, and that her clothes were cute. She copied off her mom's actions and choices. Though she thought it was wrong for her mom, she thought it was ok for her, because she was young and not married. Some of this added to the confusion in her own mind. Talking to and about the boys seemed harmless enough, but she often felt as if it wasn't as harmless as she thought. In the back of her mind she somehow knew this innocent playing was a snake in the grass. A snake that would bite her given the opportunity. She would dismiss these thoughts, saying to herself that it was just fun.

In her Sunday School class her favorite teacher talked about this kind of stuff. Miss Jean was great. Ellen felt that she was honest with her and the other girls in her class. Miss Jean would talk to them like they were friends, girls trying to live in this world the way Jesus would want them to, looking and finding truth in God's word. Wisdom to make good choices, this was what Ellen was looking for, information to be able to make choices that she wouldn't regret. Honest conversation about what the Bible says. She loved her mom, but she didn't want to wake up one morning in the same situation that Mom was in. Miss Jean would bring up a topic that related to them, then while listening to their comments would show them what the Bible said about it. It was cool to have someone take the time to show you not just what the Bible said but also how you could use it or apply it. They often talked about friends and what influence they should have in your life, if any. Or about other relationships; parents, teachers, coaches, even boys. The topics were what they were dealing with, sometimes it seemed like she knew what you were questioning that day. It helped to know the truth, if you accepted it to be truth. Ellen learned that not everyone agreed on the points that Miss Jean made. She even didn't always like the things that Miss Jean would say and point out, but one thing she did know, Miss Jean was straight with them. She wasn't just telling them things that were in some book. This was stuff she experienced or knew. She spoke with confidence and experience, like coach, Miss Jean was straight up even if you felt a little pain, you knew it was what you needed. Not like some fake know it all, but a person who had already dealt with many of these same issues. Mix that with the fact that she honestly cared about what the girls thought and it was a great class and a strong help.

Ellen started to make some of her choices by what her Mom did, and some by what her friends did, and some by what Miss Jean taught. This, at times, became confusing but it was a different confusing. It seemed that she had more tools to use. More information with which to come to a conclusion, information that she thought was good, proven. Sometimes she felt uncomfortable with her decisions though. It kind of made her feel funny when she wore something that others wore but she really didn't like, or did something because others did only to find out it really wasn't her thing. Boys were kind of like this. Her friends, especially Beth, were all about boys. They all talked and compared. They giggled at some of the things and were grossed out about others. Boys had become their favorite topic of conversation, and

Ellen loved to join in even though she had other interest. Some of her friends, Beth included, had boyfriends. They would walk together and talk on the phone. They would meet after school and on the weekends. Ellen thought about it, but when it came down to it she just wasn't wanting to hang out with a boy. However, her desire for their attention grew as her father spent more time away.

At school she would let them come up to her and talk. She loved it during lunch when everybody was hanging out together. The boys thought they were tough and cool, she thought that was dumb. She liked it more when they were funny. When it was just the girls they would compare notes and tell each other what this boy said or what this boy did. There was no official score as to prove who was liked best by the boys, but seemed like all the other girls were worried about it. Ellen was glad just to be herself and have fun.

School was almost out, and summer was coming. Ellen was looking forward to the days of more freedom. She knew that most days she could finish the things that Mom had for her to do, and then the rest of the day would be hers. By this age she could meet her friends in the park. Sometimes they would ride their bikes and sometimes just walk. Dolls and playing house were left behind. Ellen liked being a little older. She knew she wasn't an adult; but it was great that when she wanted, she could be lady-like and mature or if not, just act goofy and nobody thought it strange of her. She spent time thinking and planning what the summer would hold for her. It would be like no other summer she had ever had.

Sure enough with the longer days and increasing temperature came the end of school. It always seemed somewhat sad, yet exciting. Some friends she would see some others she wouldn't. It felt kind of crazy to be giddy and yet disappointed. She quickly put the negative out of her mind and looked square in the face of the endless possibilities of summer. Ellen looked down the three months of summer vacation as an endless time. Her first day was a complete deviation from her "normal" day. Compared to many she was out of bed early, though it was about the time she would've left to catch the bus. She dressed in full summer attire: shorts, T-shirt, flip-flops, and put her hair back in a ponytail. This was summer, and she was ready.

In the kitchen Mom was sitting at the table. Ellen kind of knew how to have the freedom that she wanted. She knew she had to find out what Mom's plan was and discuss how she could get to do what she had planned. Mom was like that. Her mom knew that Ellen was willing to help and would work hard if she knew there was an end, and she would have time for the things she wanted to do. So Mom opened up the discussion with something of an outline of what she would ask of Ellen on most days. Mom even made it flexible. Ellen was excited with the plans. Mom wanted to do some stuff together, and there was a week where they would take off and do a vacation. Mom only worked, take in work. Dad wanted her there when he came in. So this vacation would be a week that Mom did not do other people's laundry or ironing or baking. The time would be spent in the back yard bar-b-queuing, playing games, maybe running through the sprinkler. To Ellen this sounded perfect; time to spend with Mom and do things around the house she liked, and also time she could fill in herself. It was made clear to her that she would have pretty much freedom to govern herself as long as she showed herself responsible. Too cool. Do what I want, go where I want, stay out of trouble. Perfect.

This being older was great. This summer would be so different. She would even have her own money this year. The lady down the block had asked her mother if Ellen would want to clean her house once a week. Ellen would get paid for the service and would have cash to carry, so cool. Of course most of it had to go into the house fund but Mom said she could have a little of her own money. And so, freedom started. She and her friends would walk around the neighborhood and talk to people that they passed. She and Beth spent plenty of time down at the city pool. They both loved the fun they had in the sun and water, but it was made better because there were no parents around. Even her nights were a blast. She and the girls were always trading whose house they would be sleeping at. Staying up all night, junk food and soda; they never ran out of things to talk about. Mornings were hard, but worth it. This was somewhat strange for her, being able to, more or less, to decide for herself what she did and where she went.

Ellen started following her mother in styles that she wore, shorter shorts and tighter T's. There was no question that the boys noticed. She and her friends felt like the main attraction as they walked to the mall or the park. Most boys were too shy to talk to her. Only the older, cooler boys were man enough to come up to her. She loved the attention she received from the older ones. She liked it when they would talk low and bump into her. It made her feel special. Something in her stirred when the boys were around. She even felt it later when she would lie in bed and think about the day. There was something of a difference between her and her friends though. Ellen didn't like the idea of being alone with the boys. Some of her friends met with the boys and let them hang on them. She just wasn't interested in that. Looking and talking was fine, but touching was something altogether different.

She liked what Miss Jean told them, "Be careful who you let touch you, for they always leave something behind and take something with them." Ellen wasn't sure what all was meant by that, but it did help her to keep the boys at arm's length.

It wasn't all fun, though. Ellen found that sometimes after a great day, she would just crash. On the rainy days or the times when nothing was going on and she had to stay home, she would get so bummed out. The day was spent all blue, moody, and disappointed. She would find it hard to find anything to do that would hold her interest. She would try this and that, even when looking at TV she couldn't find anything that she really wanted to watch. Those days were horrible and lasted for ever. It was often on blue days that she and her mom would clash. Ellen was sure her mom didn't understand or even try to understand. She would, at times, go to her room and just cry, not even knowing why. It was hard. It would be on those days that it seemed her head would just spin. Thoughts would jump in and out, from one thing to another. It would almost make her crazy. Then like a light switch being put in the other position, everything was fine again.

The summer days shot by. So many new experiences and people. Ellen loved spending time with her friends and with her mom. For the most part her and her mom had a cool relationship. They could tell each other anything. Ellen would come home from hanging out, and she and her mom would relive the day together. Often they both would end up laughing at what the girls' escapades were that day. Her mom encouraged her interaction with the boys and at times seem to push her to get a boyfriend. Ellen began to think that her mom often wished she could do that. It added to her questions. Though she had more control over her personal time, she couldn't hold back the calendar, and before long it was time for school to start again, and her return would be completely different. High school brought its own excitement and questions.

That first day of High School was a tornado of emotions. Excitement to the point she could have exploded, then fear to point of tears. What to wear? How much time did she have left before the bus came? What would her classes be like? A constant barrage of questions with no solid, confident answers. By the time she was ready to leave the house and meet the bus, she had gained control of what at least showed on the outside. She waited desperately until the bus reached Beth's stop. Then they sat close, whispered, held hands for assurance, giggling, sharing dreams of the coming days, and most of all tried desperately to hide their nervousness. After that, they were both on their own. Beth's classes took her in one direction, Ellen's in another. They were hoping to at least have the same homeroom, but even that didn't work out. All they could do was hang on until lunch. They did share the same lunch period, for that they were very glad. Ellen had one or two classes where she saw some familiar faces, but that was little consolation. The big challenge was finding each classroom. The high school was so big and had so many more kids! There were even different buildings she had to walk to and levels to go up or down, hallways that went in every direction. It was crazy. By the time lunch rolled around, she was exhausted and only half the day was over.

The class load and homework was much more challenging. At times Ellen felt overwhelmed. She was a good student and wanted to stay that way, so she pushed herself. Algebra was definitely not her strong suit, and the teacher she had was moving way too fast for her.

It just added to her feeling of inadequacy. She just always hoped the teachers wouldn't notice her and definitely didn't want to be called on. She would sit at her desk and pay attention but looked down as much as possible. She thought if she never made eye contact with the teachers, they would leave her alone, and for the most part, it worked. She would use the time at the end of class that some teachers would give them, to start their homework. It surprised her how many of the students would talk and goof off. She just thought that they were smart and didn't need to work on it as she did. Confidence in herself was low or nonexistent. She felt so awkward and out of place. Beth said she felt the same way. This was no consolation. Neither girl put it together that if they felt that way it was likely that everyone felt that way. Ellen spent hours on her homework. She and Beth would sometimes join others and study. The only reassurance and encouragement that carried any weight was that she stayed in the A and B range when she got her papers back.

As days turned into weeks, she became more familiar with the buildings and getting from one classroom to another became much easier. There was one class, though, that she nearly had to run to in order to get there on time. She felt a little better about this when one day she saw several other students' speed walking to get to class. At least she wasn't the only one needing to hustle. The only thing that made travel more difficult was when it was raining. Then every kid had to use the halls. This seemed to greatly expand the student population, and shrink the halls. It was a mess. She was able to calm down more as she caught on to what high school teachers wanted from their students. For some of her classes she found she could stop in the hall on the way and talk to friends for a minute or two. The curriculum was still a challenge. She couldn't help it, at times she just felt stupid. The smallest thing would bother her. If she was in class writing notes and accidently dropped her pen. Oh, it would bother her for hours that others saw her be so clumsy and have to lean into the aisle and pick up her pen. It was so embarrassing. She did, though, begin to look forward to lunch and even the bus ride home. She and Beth made friends with other girls, and they all sat together in the cafeteria. They would eat, laugh, talk, make plans, and compare notes about everything from teachers to PE class to clothes, and yes, boys.

They would have these study meetings. She and Beth would set it up, and other girls would join them. It was always over at Beth's house. Ellen loved her mom, and she didn't mind that their house wasn't fancy, but it was just the fact that she never knew when her dad would show up or what shape he would be in when he did. Beth's parents always made them feel welcomed and they encouraged them in their studies. Beth's dad was even able to help with her algebra and her mom was very good at grammar. Some of the girls had the same teacher, just at different hours. Then they could help each other and study in the group. That made it much better. It helped Ellen see that she wasn't stupid, she was just normal, well, normal for her group of friends. She did like school, as did most in the group. Their study group made going to school better, because having your homework done, and a little better grasp of the information that was presented made you feel prepared and confident. That relieved a lot of stress.

Ellen thanked God for her friends, especially Beth. Jesus was becoming a big part of her life. Her mom didn't always go to church, but Ellen enjoyed the teaching, the people, and the reassurance she felt when she was there often. She knew that what she had with Jesus was so much more than rules and laws. It went way beyond religion. She knew Jesus, and He knew her. She counted on Him, and she had proven it herself that he was faithful to her. That wasn't always true with people, but that's just the way it is. People make mistakes and aren't perfect. God is perfect. She knew that God, in the name of Jesus, would always have her best in mind.

She would follow Him. That was her choice, and she liked that choice. She read her Bible to find answers and learn more of what God was like. What she heard taught in Sunday school and preached in church was the same thing that she found in the Bible. That was also reassuring. The people teaching her were trying to help her know God better. Not what they thought, but what God taught. They were helping her to be able to make good decisions and walk in God's blessing. Most of her friends didn't choose to make that connection with Jesus. At times they would asked her why she thought the way she did. Her choices and responses did put her in awkward situations at times, but Ellen accepted that. She was just being who she wanted to be. She tried to explain her relationship with Jesus to them but often they weren't interested. She so wished she could somehow show them that Jesus will help you make better choices and follow in a life with few regrets. It's just hard to explain that to someone in a way that they can understand.

When it came open, she tried out for the high school volley ball team. It was more than just a little intimidating. There were so many girls that came to that first meeting and practice. Ellen was in pretty good shape and was taught well by her other coach, so she at least wanted to try out. She changed out into her practice sweats, and as she walked toward the group she whispered a prayer asking God to help her. She ended up needing all the help she could get. The woman coach was so different from her last coach, so much more serious and really pushed them. By the end of practice there wasn't a girl who wasn't red faced and puffing. A few had just walked off. Ellen enjoyed being pushed, but even she had to keep talking to herself to keep going. She only touched a ball twice and that was to bat it to the next girl, then they were off running again. The only thing worse than the two hour practice was getting out of bed the next morning. She was so sore. Every movement was painful. She had to grit her teeth to get dressed. It was crazy; even her toes were sore. Sitting, standing, and especially walking was pure agony. All the girls were complaining and laughing about their soreness as they got dressed out for practice. Then the whistle blew, and they were back to the races again. Ellen noticed that only about half the girls showed up the second night. Coach Jill held nothing back in consideration of their sore bodies. It seemed mercy was not in her vocabulary. She pushed them like it was a Marine boot camp. Day after day fewer and fewer girls showed up. Coach hadn't had to cut any one yet. They were doing it themselves.

By the end of the week, Ellen and a few of the other girls were getting in the groove. They had caught on to the routine that Coach followed and had enough sense to prepare themselves for it. Everything was done at a dead run, after so long they were to get a drink, then back to running, hit the ball, drink, run, do it over again. They were all glad when practice was over on Friday. A two day break would be great. Then coach announced that she would be in the gym at 8:00, Saturday morning, if anyone were interested. With that, she walked away. They all knew what that meant. If you didn't show, you weren't interested in being on the team. They all groaned inside. Out in the parking lot there was some grumbling, but everyone knew they would show up. At 8:00 a.m., Coach did something different, she took roll. The girls were right in what they thought. The ones that showed would continue to work for a spot on the team; the ones that didn't would have to try again next year. After that, practice was more intense, surprise, surprise. Coach began to teach more setups and strategies. Team players were being kept on the roster to make up the team, super heroes were cut. Between practice and homework, Ellen had to stay focused to do well, so she focused.

Beth didn't like sports and didn't like that Ellen liked sports. Ellen's volleyball cut into their friend time and even their study group time. Beth sometimes would complain to Ellen about her practice and how much time she spent with the team. Ellen really didn't know how to respond to this. She never wanted to hurt Beth's feelings, and it wasn't intentional not to spend time with her, but Ellen truly loved the challenge and the adventure of pushing herself. The team was like a family, not to leave Beth out but to add to Ellen's life. She wanted both, but Beth didn't see it that way. It broke Ellen's heart, but Beth started to pull away from her, and there didn't seem to be anything she could do about it. The few times they would be together, Beth would poke fun at their differences; sports, parents, homes, even church. It seemed the harder she tried, the wider the gap between them became. There were nights of tears at how things had changed. She never imagined that she and Beth wouldn't be together and close.

This put a completely new spin in Ellen's life. She had interacted with Mom and Dad, and friends. She had come to like and relate to teachers, coaches, and people from church; but this was different. She would find herself thinking about what she thought Beth was thinking about her. This was a little new. What people thought, and how they felt about her was becoming more important to her. She wanted the team to think she was good and a dependable player. She wanted Beth to like her and feel like they were sisters. She wanted boys to think she was cute. She wanted her mom to think she was growing up and being responsible, to feel she could trust her. It made for a hard time, always trying to make sure everyone thought something good about you, but that seemed to be the right thing to do. She felt that the Bible taught her to do the right thing, and that people should see you as a good person. It seemed she was the one hurt and bothered when she felt she let someone down. She hated that feeling. Relationships started being more complicated. There was this pressure to measure up and to be what everyone wanted you to be.

Ellen noticed that these new feelings also affected how she looked at others. There were certain girls at school that she just didn't like. The way they acted or dressed. Some of them hung all over the boys. She didn't like how they always got all the attention. Sometimes she wouldn't let it bother her, and sometimes, wow, look out, she would just be steaming mad because something didn't go the way she thought it should. Ellen had noticed before, and now it was even more obvious, what it would take to catch the attention of the boys. Even though when she and her friends would talk about having a boyfriend, she really wasn't interested, she still wanted their attention. Beth was over board boy crazy. It was her only topic of conversation. This was another wedge between her and Ellen. Beth had before, begged Ellen to go with her to meet boys or to talk to them on the phone. She would make Ellen feel like she was letting her down if she did go along. Ellen made Beth swear that she wouldn't give any of the boys her phone number. Beth and the other girls would laugh at her and make fun of her. It hurt Ellen's feelings to be on the outside. So little by little she began to bend. Ellen wanted to be Beth's best friend. So she began hanging out with Beth and some boys on Saturdays. They would meet at the mall and hang out. She gave Bobby her phone number, and they would talk. She liked him, and they had a good time together. She followed Beth's lead and dressed the way the boys liked. She looked into the full length mirror one day after getting dressed and much to her surprise and delight she noticed new curves and bumps, no wonder that the boys are looking, she thought pridefully. Even though she was often uncomfortable in shorter skirts and tight shirts, Ellen didn't want to disappoint Bobby or make Beth think she wasn't cool. She grew to accept Bobby holding her hand and putting his arm around her. His attention and closeness made her feel loved and secure. Increasingly, though, there were times that she would be bored on the phone with him; and often she was wishing to just wear jeans and a hoody. Her interest in this boyfriend/girlfriend stuff was dissolving. The stirring that she felt inside started to wain as his attention was more on her body and less on her as a person. It reminded her of what her Dad said to her when she was 10. So on the day he tried to kiss her the world changed.

5

The last several months of school went by in a flash. Ellen broke up with Bobby, to her great relief, for which she paid dearly with Beth. But at that point she didn't have the opportunity to explain herself well to her. With the end of the volley ball season, came post season games. It was exciting to be a part of something that worked so well, but this also made her schedule crazier than usual and caused her grades to suffer. They did make it through the third round, then lost. It was disappointing, yet in a way Ellen was glad it was over. Exciting yes, but also stressful. She could now concentrate on her class work. This, again, was an obstacle between her and Beth. Ellen spent time in prayer asking God what she should do, seeking guidance on what He wanted her to place as the important thing. She felt that he showed her she should push everything else aside and look at what it would take to finish well in all her classes. With that goal in mind, she focused on it, leaving little to no time for goofing off or her special friend. It wasn't that she neglected Beth on purpose. It was that school took the priority position. The distance between them continued to grow. By finals week, Ellen had pulled her grades back up and was confident going into her exams. Beth no longer showed up at the bus stop. Her boyfriend picked her up in his car. Even at lunch the couple sat together leaving Ellen to her studies. It seemed that the two of them had become so different and they couldn't get back to where they were. Ellen even wondered if Beth wanted too. She was all about that guy, and in Ellen's eye she was so much more than him. Not condemning to him but seeing Beth's value and character. It was obvious to Ellen that he really didn't appreciate her for who she was. It was like Beth had given self out cheap, not waiting for the best that God had for her. It was very concerning for Ellen, but she knew at this point in their relationship there was nothing she could do in person so she increased her prayers.

When the last day of school finally arrived, Ellen had taken no time to plan for the coming summer. She slept in late her first Saturday home. Then spent much of the day working around the house and talking with her mom. Ellen had been so wrapped up with school that she and her mom had a lot of catching up to do. Her mom understood her commitment and diligence to her school work, and they talked about why others didn't understand, namely Beth. The conversation jumped around to many different topics, most of which were tied to relationships. Her Mom admitted that she wasn't very good in that area, but Ellen had confidence in her good heart and experience. Her Mom didn't understand the way she thought about boys and her lack of interest in having a boyfriend. Often throughout the day Ellen had tears in her eyes over Beth, and friends, and different confusions that she felt. Even though she had slept in late that morning she went to bed early feeling exhausted. Lying in bed Beth turn to the place she always felt comfort, though maybe questions still remained, those nights of silent prayers in the dark, talking to God on such a personal level, working her way through the tears and to the place where she at least felt some relief. Then sleep would overtake her.

Sunday brought a new, fresh outlook for her. The discussion she and her Mom shared had brought some new light and clarity. She dressed for church and heartily encouraged her mom to come with her, but she refused. In Sunday school her favorite teacher, Miss Sara, talked about relationships, almost as if she had been in her room last night while Ellen talked to God. She pointed out how God was all about relationship. Love God and love others. Several times what the teacher said hit a cord, and Ellen started writing things down. After class there wasn't much time before she had to get into the church auditorium. She did, though, ask Miss Sara if she could meet with her and talk more on this topic of relationships. The teacher was very interested in meeting with her, and as they both headed for a place to sit in church, set up a time to meet later in the week. After the service was over Miss Sara, came to her very excited. She told Ellen that a few ladies met for Bible study on Tuesday and asked if she would like to join them. They all could look at relationships, what the Bible says about it, and what they have experienced. Ellen thought it would be cool and agreed. She was very much looking forward to the meeting, and when she arrived back home she invited her mom. Ellen was not surprised when she declined. Mom was a sometimes show up, sit in the back, don't talk to anyone, church goer. Ellen tried to show her how much better life could be if lived with Jesus in the middle of it. Mom would have none of it. Ellen easily recalled who first taught her about God and Jesus. Ellen knew that her own relationship with God was brought to her and taught to her by her Mom. Now she would just say Jesus didn't fit her lifestyle. Ellen's pat answer to that was, 'He doesn't fit any one's lifestyle, our lives need to fit Him.' She just wanted her Mom to have what she had. Mom was always searching, looking, not really happy any more. She knew Jesus could bring some contentment in her life.

Tuesday came and Ellen met with the ladies from church. It was awkward at first, they were all older and had kids, some of their children were her age. After every one said hi, they prayed to open, and then the ladies started talking. They didn't push Ellen to join in but she felt welcome to do so if she wanted. The discussion was active. They all had experiences that they shared, many were mistakes that they made, and advice about how to avoid making those same ones. What they made clear was relationships need our attention no matter how old we are, being sure that you thought before you moved, and that there are no experts. God and the Bible were the best guide. One shared that she had to learn the balance between trying to please people, and letting them push her into things she didn't want to do. Her comment was that she finally realized that if people really care about you they won't push you, and pleasing others should never override pleasing

God. Miss Sara talked about her first boy/girl relationship and what she faced. Ellen could really relate when she told how she didn't want a boyfriend at that time but felt pressure to have one since, of course, her best friend had one. Miss Sara went on and gave more details that made it sound like Ellen herself was telling the story. She liked the guy, he was nice and fun but it just really didn't interest her; friends yes, boyfriend no. Ellen couldn't hold back any longer. Slowly she started to share about her relationship. It was awkward and uncomfortable. Miss Sara questioned if Ellen felt like it was forced, like she had to work to want to be with him. Ellen agreed with great relief. She had not talked to people who understood the way she felt. Another older woman brought up how people we hang around influence us. She recounted how a group of friends she had greatly influenced her choice of clothes. In a few years she realized that she really didn't like that style and went back to being herself. This woman pointed out that no one pushed or talked her into the different style, just being around them drew her into that direction. She is still friends with many of that group, and loves them greatly, and her hair style and the clothes she wears really don't matter to them at all. They all laughed. One of the ladies said she wished someone would have told her that it wasn't her responsibility to find the right man for her. She had heard and believed that if a person will wait for God, He will bring the right person to you. Ellen asked how a person will know when that happens. The ladies, all, almost at the same time, smiled and said, 'don't worry, you'll know'. They all laughed again. The meeting felt good, it was relaxed and opened. The conversation just kept going. There was no leader or director it was a group of people sharing things that might be helpful to one another. Ellen really never said much but listened with great interest and loved the atmosphere. Finally one of them said it was late, they prayed together for God's help to work within their own relationships and went home.

Ellen walked home at a pace that offered her time to think about what everyone had said. A lot had been said and to her it was stuff that she wanted and needed. The women she had met with, in her opinion, were ladies. Individuals that she would want to grow up to be like; fun, friendly, women that were confident and comfortable with who they were, even with the mistakes that they had made. Ellen kept thinking. She was sure that God put these women in her life to learn from. She wanted to remember everything that was said. They showed her how to have balance with friends, set her own pace with boys, and be herself. One of the challenges that she now faced, was to define who, "herself" was. That thought made her stop. That would be a good idea. She should think about what kind of person, what kind of a woman, she would want to be. Ellen thought to herself that if she thought it through she could then make decisions that would enable her and move her into a positon to be the person she wanted to be. All the ladies had different good things that Ellen wanted to add to her life, but all of them had one thing good in common, that was their relationship with Jesus. That's where she would start, her choices would all be made with Jesus as her perspective. She would make a list of the qualities that she saw in these ladies and others, make sure that they line up with what the Bible says about Jesus, and then make them a part of her life. She thought if she did this she would know what kind of a person she wanted to be and even have answers before the questions would come up. Ellen started thinking of the things she should put on her list. She was very glad that so many of the qualities she thought of, her mother showed also. It wasn't that the ladies at the meeting were better than her Mom, it was that her Mom seemed to trade who she wanted to be for who she was. Ellen thought that maybe it is hard to become who you want to be without Jesus.

When she arrived at home she went to her room to begin to write down as much of what was talked about as she could remember. This was going to be the first step in making here list, which she called 'steps for life'. She had been told many times to just keep putting one step in front of the other, so if each step was directed towards God they would be the perfect 'steps for life'. Over time she would work on this. Noting things that she had heard said, what she saw in other women she admired, and her 'steps for life' list, Ellen began to write down how to have these same things come alive in her life. Her 'steps for life' would say things like, be yourself. Then under that she would fill in; wear simple, modest clothes that make you feel good and look good, for you. Another one was, date when you are ready; no pressure, God will provide and prove Himself trustworthy, should come easy, no hurry. One of her favorites was, prepare for the future; invest in friends, go the extra mile, work very hard in school, keep learning and enjoying all types of relationships, save some money. She would revisit the list, often adding to it or changing items. It seemed to be more useful with more descriptions of how to accomplish the goals or examples of what accomplishment would look like.

Her summer continued to go by. This was the busiest she had ever been. With the passing of her last birthday she acquired her driver's license, real freedom. With that she started a 'real' job. The schedule was challenging because between her and Mom there was only one car. They worked together to make it possible for both of them to accomplish all the things that needed to be done. Sometimes Ellen would have to ride the bus and wait around until work started. Her Mom at times would leave early for her appointments and drop Ellen off, and so on. They communicated well and stayed flexible. Both of these qualities were added to Ellen's 'steps for life' communicate well and stay flexible. The job was fun and Ellen loved the work and the people she worked with were a blast. She still tried to call Beth at least once a week, but by this time Beth just continued to blow her off. She would never come to the phone. Often after calling, Ellen would cry, because she missed Beth so much. Sometimes Ellen would go over to Beth's house to see if she could catch up with her that way. While there, she would spend time with Beth's parents. They were so very close. Ellen had spent a lot of time in their home and had grown to love them both. Beth's Dad filled a place that was very empty in her life. He would still give Ellen a hug, and when they talked he would look right into her eyes. It made her feel loved, accepted, important, and respected.

During all this busyness Ellen took several weekends to attend volleyball camps. These weekends were worse than any of the coaches she had ever had, combined! They would pack a month's worth of training into two and half days. It was nuts. She didn't think that she would be a professional volleyball player but it was on steps of life list to get to college and she knew to do it she would need a scholarship, they give scholarships to volleyball players. When she found that because of their financial status she could attend some of these camps for free, it was a no brainer. She was working to follow the path that Jesus opened to her and had called her to. Prayer was her constant companion.

Into this whirlwind of events Ellen's Dad walked back into the house. He seemed meaner than before and the way he looked at her made her feel creepy. He interrupted their setup with the car and getting around. Ellen was late for work on a few days. She couldn't understand why he just didn't leave them alone. Her Mom melted into herself. Ellen hated it and started hating him. Then she looked at her steps for life and saw where she wrote, we can't control how others treat us only how we treat others. The pain they cause hurts them also, so keep in your mind who you are and who God is. Love one another. She was then determined not to hate her Dad. Who was this man really and how did he get to this point. She tried several times to talk to him but he just looked her up and down in that creepy way and walked away. With her last attempt he called her some foul names, talked about her body, and told her to shut up. He walked out and never came back. She felt sorry for him. Many days and nights she remembered him in her prayers. As usual after a few days of being gone her happy-go-lucky Mom came back. Ellen felt sorry for her as well and was determined not to allow her Dad to control her like that. She prayed for them both.

Back at work there were always boys who were trying to impress her and get her attention. She felt that to enjoy their company at work and stay open was ok. That way God could lead her but would not make her seem unfriendly or rude. She found so many of them just very immature, goofy. They would brag about the silliest things and act tough around the other boys. It seemed to her as they tried so hard to act cool or tough they couldn't be themselves and it made them look like foolish little boys. That was it, she was looking for potential men, those that will grow into good men. Someone who could make a tough decision and do what it would take to see it through. All she kept seeing was boys who were going to be boys, they seemed to be lacking. She had no problem working with them, laughing and talking, but the minute they tried to act all serious and possibly ask her on a date, she was done. They had nothing to offer. Her favorite times were when they, boys and girls, were working together. As a team striving to reach the finish line. Encouraging one another, helping were needed, joking and joshing back and forth, but still working and pushing, with effort to accomplish something that needed to be done. It was only then that she would see something of a glimpse in some of the boys, something that may have potential. Then poof, it would be gone. Even with the busyness of the summer she was already focused on the coming year of school. Good grades was the priority, but she was going to be killer on the volleyball court!

6

Ellen had the misconception that by the middle of her junior year of high school she would have a better handle on life, maybe more confidence, more answers. That didn't seem to be the case. She still constantly felt challenged and inadequate. Striving to keep up and do well. That was one of her steps of life, don't just do it, apply yourself with effort to do it well. But she was beginning to feel like she was always over analyzing every choice; which is best, which way do I go, does it even matter, is that bad, good, or ok. Second guessing herself had become so common. Disappointed on how things kept working out. Feeling like she should have done this instead of that. The yucky feeling that people were talking about her or noticing every imperfection. After she would get finished talking to someone she would run the conversation over and over in her mind. Thinking of what she said and what they said and what did they mean by this or that. What did they think of what she said? Even fighting the battle of wanting to stand out in a crowd yet not be noticed, such conflicting feelings. Relationships haunted her. The relationship that consumed so many of her thoughts was her friendship with Beth, but right with that one was her Dad. They hadn't seen him in months and she thought that it may be her fault. She didn't know what she could do in either case and it made her feel bad, real bad at times. Sometime she really didn't like who she was. She finally asked Miss Sara from church for some of her time to talk about it.

When they came together Miss Sara had invited some of the other ladies from church that were at the first meeting. Ellen was thrilled that they would all come together for her, that they were interested, and cared. Their smiles and attitudes made her feel comfortable and willing to open up. She shared what she had done and even showed them her 'steps for life' which now she had in a notebook. They were stunned. They all admitted that what she had done was a fantastic idea. Something everyone should do, and admitting that none of them ever had or had even thought of it. They were all very encouraging to her. In their excitement they asked a myriad of questions. The conversation went on for some time, then Miss Sara realize there was something else on her mind, asked Ellen what was really concerning her. With that they let Ellen share with them her problems. They all listened very intently and let her go all the way through her thoughts. She told them of the challenge to apply what she had laid out in her steps of life. Telling them that it seemed like there was never a question that had a simple answer. Even talking about how often that her mind would wonder into thinking about stuff she knew was not good. Things, that when she caught herself, she would ask herself why she was thinking that. Like thinking poorly about her Mom and numbering all her Mom's problems and faults, doing the same thing to friends and teacher. These thoughts she was talking about were always negative and she didn't want to be thinking poorly about others or tempting herself to be prideful or judgmental. Then she began to tell how poorly she at times felt about herself and who she was. Walking around with little or no confidence, feeling uncomfortable around others. Then went on to her friend Beth and how much that hurt, and her Dad and all the confusion that went with that.

When she stopped the ladies started looking at each other and kind of smiling. Ellen began to get embarrassed, maybe she shared too much? Maybe they were thinking she was a horrible person? The silence became very awkward. Ellen was thinking about getting up and running out. She thought she was going to cry. What was probably only a few seconds felt to her to be hours? Then Miss Sara started with her opinion and then each of the ladies added in their own points or feelings. They all shared that they too have felt the same way. These types of challenges are not overcome by age or time or even practice. They encouraged her with the information that if she is questioning how to act or react to life, she is growing in Christ and desiring to follow Him. One of them asked if she questioned these things two years ago, to which Ellen replied she didn't. So then they helped her to see that her effort to do the right thing, the better thing, was a sign of maturity and growth in the Lord. Ellen began to see their point and began to feel some relief come over her. One of the ladies pointed out that some people think that when you strive to walk with Jesus that life gets easier and how that really wasn't true. It was explained to her like this. As we strive to live a life that is in the character of Christ we add to our lives things such as responsibility, compassion, concern, obedience, and so on. These are to be added to our lives, but they are contrary to our sinful nature. All children must be taught to share, be nice, and obey. As we grow and mature we learn to add responsibility, truth, diligence, and things like that. It is an on-going process. As we mature we face many different choices that will call us to consider the consequences of each action taken. We begin to realize how many, if not all of our choices, affect the lives of others. This does and should apply a little pressure, it is the reality of the weight of our decisions, but the Bible says to be strong in the Lord and in the power of his might. They then went on to look at thoughts. Thinking poorly about people, mentally complaining about parents and teachers, thinking inappropriately about others, here again they all just laughed and said join the club. They all confessed to fighting against the same things. One of the ladies laughed and said at least you don't yet have a husband to add to your list yet. This information really brought Ellen some hope. She had begun to think she was just a horrible person and definitely not a good Christian. It was great hearing this stuff. It was great being with these ladies. It was wonderful that they would share their failures, successes, and ideas. Then they turned their attention to the topic of relationships. These will always be a challenge. They asked some questions about Beth and then about her Dad. Not digging or pushing, kind of just general questions that could give them an idea of what Ellen was facing. Miss Sara said that you can't force people to like you or come along side you. Another of the women mentioned that we must work at relationships and offer forgiveness but we're not responsible if the person doesn't accept it. One lady mentioned something that touched Ellen deeply. Jesus never wants to demotivate you. He is in the business to lift you up. It is the world that will knock you down. Let Jesus lift you up to keep trying. They all had a time of prayer together and then went home. When Ellen started her Mom's car to drive home she felt revved up to keep trying.

Things didn't change much. Questions continued to come, relationships continued to be a challenge, and decisions had to be made. The difference Ellen could see was how she faced them. She accepted the fact that if she wanted to be the full person she wanted to be it was going to take commitment and dedication. She would dedicate each day to Jesus and work on that day and plan for tomorrow. Ellen began to feel more positive about who she was. She was enjoying who she was becoming. She could even see how it affected others. Her up, positive attitude touched the people around her. When she would come flying into the house, rush to get to work, or volleyball practice, or study group, the smile on her face and the apparent light-heartedness in her life, made her Mom and others smile. The influence was clear. Her Mom quit the flirting, and trashy dressing, and the attention-getting tactics towards other men. They were able to talk more about what God was doing in their lives. Often they went to church together and even Sunday school at times. The people at work included her more, she was a part of the group and not just a member of the work team. She even had some of them ask her what happened to her? What made the change? Ellen was excited to tell people what Jesus had led her to do in her life. Her boss noticed that she was more focused and responsible. It made her feel good being known as a good worker. He even paid her more to help him do some of the bookwork and ordering things. He put her in charge of organizing the products. The extra money was a blessing. By this time Ellen was helping her Mom pay the bills, less and less was coming in from her Dad.

There were some draw backs though. Some of her old friends didn't understand or like the change that they saw in Ellen. They would just walk by her, not even saying hi. Even if she walked up to them it was very awkward. This was most true with Beth. It was a continual disappointment to her. Ellen missed Beth so very much. It was so strange to go to the study group that they both started and see almost all new faces. Oh she still had some of her old friends, but with every year more and more pull away from school and studying and more into boys and partying. She missed the days of staying up all night talking with her gang of girls. Going to the park and acting silly. Walking in the mall, shopping, sharing an order of fries, and telling each other what was on their hearts. She had friends and she enjoyed herself but it was not like when it was with her and Beth. She wondered if she would ever find another friend like her. Another issue was her schedule. She seemed to always be running and worrying that she wasn't going to get everything done or be on time for things. Ellen often felt she was missing out. When she was at work or the study group she knew that there were other things she could be doing. Football games, parties, even school dances were missed in the name of responsibility and commitments. As the school year came to an end this became more apparent. Everyone was talking about the summer coming up and what they would be doing. Vacations, pool side, running around. Ellen, well, her boss offered her a full time position that would also give her overtime. She was all excited when he gave her the job, then dropped like a rock when she realized that it would consume all of her summer time fun. She just kept telling herself that it was worth it and will pay off in the end. Life asked for responsibility and work. Either you accept it or you hold yourself back from growing up and becoming a steady, dependable, mature adult.

She could see the benefits, and there were many. Honor roll at school, the raise she received at work, more freedoms at home, all of these showed the advantage to a life live for Christ in this manner. Ellen was convinced that these choices made her feel better about herself and avoided other unpleasureable things. She knew that there was less stress in having all her homework completed and done well. There were no worries about someone finding out something she did that was wrong, or being caught in a lie. She greatly enjoyed that her boss trusted her and was very pleased with the work she did. Still there were times that she would have to argue with herself. It seemed that it would be easier to live like everyone else and let things slide and do just enough to get by. It was so inviting to follow her friends and run around and party and let the chips fall where they may. Most of them seemed to be getting by just fine. Ellen would find herself trying to understand why she kept pushing herself, until the day she analyzed the words she used to describe these lives that she envied; an easier life, letting things slide, enough to get by, let the chips fall where they may. She in no way wanted to be known for any of those things. It wasn't so much what others thought or said about her but her opinion of who she was. She desired to live up to her full potential, nothing less. It was clear that a better, fuller life came to those who gave themselves and applied what was needed to experience the doors that would be open.

Time went by as time does. One school year melted into the summer which gave way to the next school year. Ellen's junior year had ended up proving to be much better. Her grades stayed up there, and volleyball played out as she planned. Summer had flown by in a flash and now she was heading into her senior year. She thought the world would change, and it would, making that quite an understatement.

7

By the end of the summer Ellen was crazy with excitement. This would be her senior year, they would own the school. No more wondering where a room was or if she could get to class on time or this or that started. They had been there for three years and they knew how it all worked. She had already registered and set up her classes for the coming year. Coach had assured her that she had a great shot for a scholarship. With that in mind she set her goal to keep her GPA up and finish courses that would help her in the degree she was moving towards. She had taken the time off for one volleyball camp just to stay in shape and sharp. She felt ready. Her boss knew that school came first with her and that she would be starting college in the fall. He wanted to help her succeed, it was his plan that this was a move for the future for both of them. He talked to her about her schedule and planned to cut her hour's way back compared to what she had been working. Mom even joined in and adjusted the budget for a future with a lower income. She and Ellen understood what it would take to make it work and they proved on paper that they, together, could make it on less, so they would. It seemed that all the ducks were in a row and ready to be herded into her senior year. So cool.

The first day of school was just fun. Seeing people that you haven't seen all summer and catching up, a far cry from four years ago when she couldn't find her classes, ran to get to class, and just wanted to cry. Talking and joking, acting like they owned the place, living out the whole senior on campus life style. Class time was nothing like that. Ellen was all work and serious. She had taken classes that were prep classes for college, some were college level classes. She was going to need to be very focused and dedicated. That was ok. She could do it, and thought that if she paid her dues now it would pay off in the end. Even the bus ride on the first day was good. She rode the bus to save money. She looked at it as more friend time. The only drawback to the day was the absence of Beth. They no longer ran in the same circles and Beth hadn't ridden the bus in what seemed to be forever. Even over the last weeks of summer they never crossed paths. Ellen had dreamed that maybe they would share a class or a lunch hour but that was not the case. It wasn't just disappointing, she missed her best friend desperately. She was determined to see her in the next few days.

When Thursday had passed and they hadn't passed in the hall Ellen made up her mind to go by her house, like she was stopping to visit with her parents, and see if she could catch her at home. She did and the surprise was on both of them. Ellen stayed on the bus and waited for Beth's stop to come up. She knew it without question with so many years of being at each other's houses, it was almost natural. When the bus stopped she got off, she walked around the block to the house she felt was her second home. There, sitting on the porch, was Beth. Ellen called as she started up the walk, and then she noticed, Beth was going to have a baby. They met each other at the top of the stairs, caught in a stare, then with tears, they hugged. It had been so long. They both had missed each other so very much. The past couple of years melted away and they sat down to talk like they had never been apart. They would say a few words then hug and say a few words, laugh, cry, and hug. Different choices had been made and opposite paths had been taken but they were still the same girls who were bonded together by something so much more that the word friendship could ever encompass. From a window Beth's Mom watched and cried herself, seeing something for which she had hoped and prayed for so very long.

Then the conversation turned serious. The tears went from joy to regret and fear. Ellen honored her friend by giving her full attention and listening with love and no judgement or condemnation. Beth had hooked up with a senior when she and Ellen were sophomores. He and Beth did everything together. Her parents didn't like him. They had tried to make her see that she was so much more than him. Lovingly they talked to her about what they could and couldn't see in him, their concerns. But she thought he was so cool. He said the nicest things, always picked her up for school, and took her places on dates. She looked at Ellen and said he looked me in the eye and told me he loved me, I believed him and thought I felt the same way. Their relationship kept moving forward at a breakneck pace but she had held him off when he wanted her to do more when they were alone and making out. She knew it was wrong, she felt that he was wrong, at times she didn't even like him. But something kept her seeing him, wanting him. She went on to share that he told her that he was tired of waiting for her to give him more and share their love, and he dropped her. Beth was devastated for months while he ignored her and went out with other girls. Beth never hesitated, it was like a shook up can of hot soda, once it was opened she just let it all come out. She told Ellen that she wanted to call her and even dialed the phone one time but thought Ellen wouldn't understand. One time when Ellen came over Beth had stayed in her room while she visited with her parents, wanting Ellen's friendship and help but just not able to ask. Beth looked down to tell the rest of the story. After four months he called her and told her how much he missed her and needed to see her. He couldn't stop thinking about her and just had to see her. "It was everything I wanted to hear." She jumped at the opportunity, and they got together. It was so exciting to have the opportunity to see him again, and he sounded so sincere. To be back in his car, sitting next to him, smelling his cologne. It was a dream come true. It was what I had been waiting for, she had told herself. We rode around for about an hour and then he pulled into the back of the school parking lot. Beth had tears running down her face. She didn't blame him totally, though he was lying and being manipulative. They started kissing and just kept going. Now Beth had to stop for a while. When she started again she told of how rough he had been and how unfeeling it was. She hated the memory. That was the last time he called her. Beth shared that their paths did cross once, and she told him that she was pregnant, he just laughed and walked away. She was crushed. Even now she was so confused. How could he have said all those things to her? How could she have been so blind, so foolish? Though it had been 6 months since she found out, and she could no longer fit into her jeans, she still couldn't believe it. With no plan and no direction, the feeling of being lost was so real. Ellen could hear the despair in her voice and see the fear in her eyes.

There is nothing an 18 year old girl can say to her peer that would speak security and hope for her and her baby's future. Ellen knew that there was only one step for Beth to take in order to start moving in a positive direction. Ellen told Beth that she loved her and would be her friend forever. They both sat back on the porch swing in silence and watched the traffic go by. Beth reached over to hold Ellen's hand while they were swinging back and forth. Time and emotions went by. Confidence came from somewhere deep inside when Ellen began to speak.

"Beth, this may not be what you or I thought would be our future but I'll tell you one thing, I'm not going to let the past set our direction or feelings about the future."

"What are you talking about?"

"Beth," they turned to face each other, "a baby should be exciting and fun. What do your parents think about this?"

"They have been talking more like what you are saying. They have put the past behind them and are looking forward to being grandparents. I just can't get over disappointing them in this way."

"Ok, I think the first way to make better decisions in the future is to get rid of the guilt and regret of the past. Then you'll be able to think clear and make good choices. Do you agree with that?"

"Yes, there is no doubt that everything is clouded and confused. What do I do?"

"Take the same step I did. Realize that there is a God and He has a plan for your life and the life of your baby. It was my opinion a few years ago that I was going my own way. Making my own choices, and some of them weren't the best for me though I knew Jesus I really wasn't following Him. Somebody told me He could forgive me of my past, remove the guilt, and help me follow the plan that God had for me. At that time in my life I was scared and confused. I didn't like what was happening and saw no way out. So I just told God, 'I'm a mess God, but if you'll help me I'll try it your way.' That night I kept telling God all the junk I had in my life and every bad decision I had made. I told Him I wanted Jesus to forgive my sins so I could start over, and He did."

"I don't understand that, how do you know he forgave your sins?"

"I couldn't be more positive if someone handed me a piece of paper or sent me a text. You couldn't convince me any more if you had God stand in front of me and tell me, 'your sins are forgiven.' It's one thing to hold or hear a declaration, it's totally something else to feel the truth of the declaration. I know that Jesus forgave me on that day and continues to forgive me of my sins. He takes the junk out of the way so I can make better decision."

Ellen stopped talking and gave Beth a minute. They continued to swing. There was so much being said in the silence, neither girl wanted to miss a word. It was Beth that spoke first.

"I know I need something. There is no question that I need help. I've messed up my life and now I've messed up someone else's life." She stopped, she put her face into her hands and cried. Ellen was about to reach for her when she continued to speak, praying outload. "Father I know I've sinned. I know that I've messed up so much. I'm sorry, I'm really sorry. I need you to forgive me so I can start over. I need help and you're the only one that can do it. Please God forgive me and change my life. I'm so sorry. This baby had no choice and he or she deserves a good Mom. Please help me. I can't be a child raising a child, I need you to help me be a Mom raising a child. I pray in the name of your

Son Jesus. Ellen told me one time that Jesus paid the price for my sins. So in Jesus name I pray. I hope I did this right. Thank you God." They both just sat there. The world stopped. It seemed that nothing moved nor anytime past. Life was changing with no sign, just silence. Seconds pasted like days and no one missed a thing. Finally Beth looked up. She leaned slightly and Ellen hugged her. Beth let out a deep breath. Then they both sat up and started talking again.

Beth had a million questions and the conversation jumped all over. In the middle of one of her sentences Beth giggled and said "I just feel so much better," then she grabbed her belly, laughing and said "so does she." They both laughed. When the laughter died down Beth went on, "No really. For the first time in months I feel relief. I know God has forgiven me. I have no doubts that he is now with me and will help me. It must be Him, because I feel that I can. I can plan ahead, and be excited."

Ellen shared, "I love being around others that have a relationship with God. My problems, your problems, they don't just disappear, but the huge difference is knowing you have God to help you face them. Together we'll help each other keep that perspective. God's in control, has a plan for our lives, and He will help us to follow the best path for us. It's so cool, so real, Jesus is our Savior."

The girls continued to talk till the sun was going down. Beth's Mom could stand it no longer. She came out on to the porch and joined the girls. She encouraged Ellen to stop and call her Mom to tell her where she was. Beth's parents had supper for the four of them, it felt like old times as they all talked and even played a board game together. They all laughed through the evening but with school the next day Ellen had to go. At the door the two of them hugged again. When they separated they were both crying again. They laughed at each other and parted. Ellen felt like she floated home. When she opened the door to their home she was exhausted. The house was dark so she went straight to bed planning on telling everything to her Mom in the morning. When she laid her head down on her pillow she prayed and thanked God for coming into Beth's life and saving her. Now they were spiritual sisters, both in the family of God. Ellen continued to thank Him for bringing Beth some relief in her worries. Somewhere in her prayers she fell asleep.

The school year clicked by. At times her classes were difficult. Ellen was in two study groups and still at times asked for extra help. This effort kept her grades up where she wanted them. Beth was doing school from home, because she still had a hard time being around others. Volleyball was coming up so Ellen was trying to get some conditioning in. She still worked as much as she could, since they needed the money. Ellen enjoyed work. It was a place where she felt confident and comfortable. She had been there long enough that she knew what needed to be done and how to get it done. The people that she worked with were mostly fun to be with and hard workers as well. People came and went and there was always someone being trained. Ellen did most of the training, it was part of her responsibility, which was often challenging. Her boss was good at picking good people, which really helped; and it helped Ellen become a good communicator. Training the new people was helpful in the fact that she also did a lot of the scheduling. Since she knew what they could do and what they still needed to learn, she could cover the work needing to be done with the right people to do it. And the year continued to pass by.

The time came for Beth to have her baby. Ellen was so excited. Beth's Mom kept texting her all day long to keep her up with the progress. Everything went fine. Beth had a rough delivery but the baby finally came, Mom and baby were so beautiful. Ellen was so surprised that she had a girl. Beth always said it was going to be a girl; she just knew. She named the little girl Josephine Ellen, they would call her JoE. Josephine after Beth's Mother and Ellen after her best friend. Ellen was speechless, and tears welled up in her eyes when she heard the news. Beth always addressed Ellen as Aunt Ellen when she was around the baby. Ellen was so proud. It showed that Beth planned that she would be a part of the baby's life. Beth had grown and matured so much in her faith. She and Ellen often had Bible study and prayer together. They were accountable to one another for their walk with Christ and the responsibilities in each other's lives. It was very helpful for them both, that they didn't feel like they were out there by themselves. They had been praying for the baby for months and now they continued to do so. Life never fails to add new experiences and opportunities.

Beth's life was so different. It was no more me, my, and mine. It was all us and her. Beth at first had to force herself to always put the baby first then, in a short time, it just came naturally, and that made her feel better about herself and that JoE was getting what she needed. Beth continued to pray that God would make her a good Mom. Not just right now but in the future. There still were so many questions to face and decisions to be made, along with the many needs of a new born. At times she would get so tired. The baby didn't always sleep at night. She was still trying to finish school. There was nothing wrong with a GED, but Beth wanted a diploma from her High School. That was a goal she set. Ellen had shown her that goals are good and now she agreed. She was determined to take care of her school work, take care of JoE, and take care of their future. All with God's help.

8

When volleyball started an old challenge grew into a pretty good size problem, transportation. Ellen used the school bus, the city bus, walking, even riding her bike, but her responsibilities kept growing and the distances to cover were becoming greater. Ellen didn't feel as if she was taking on more but the things she had already committed to were growing. She and Beth were praying to find an answer but as of yet nothing changed, until one Saturday morning, a stranger knocked on the door of their home.

He introduced himself as a friend of her Dads. Mom had answered the door and let him in, although quite reluctantly. However, time proved him to be honest and genuine. Mom vaguely remembered him from a past meeting when Dad and she used to spend time together around others. When the introductions were done and he had sat down, he began mumbling and stuttering, trying to find words that couldn't be found. He finally looked Mom in the eyes and said that Dad had died some five or six months ago. Trying to soften the blow, the man said something about an accident. The work he did was dangerous. It was a terrible thing.

Ellen was numb. The room was still and became close and stuffy. Sure she hadn't seen her Dad in a very long time, but she never thought he would have died. When her thoughts came back to the man in the room, he was handing her Mom the keys to the car out front. The title was in the glove box and already had her name on it.

He got up to leave saying something about his ride waiting, desperate to get out of the very awkward situation. He stopped at the door. "I know that he was a jerk. I never understood why he did what he did, but he always had a place in his life for both of you. This proves it. The cars in your name, and there's some stuff in the back seat you both need to go through." He turned and closed the door behind him.

Ellen and her Mom just stood there staring at the door trying to understand what they were told. Tears rolled down both their faces, and they embraces one another. The news was such a shock that they leaned on one another for support. In the silence of a home where such sadness invades, hours pass without notice. At some point it was like the both of them looked up and noticed that the sun had gone down, and they were now sitting on the couch together in almost complete darkness. Mom wanted to take a walk and invited Ellen to go with her. It was cold, so they bundled up and went out. Block by block they strolled, sometimes in silence, and sometimes talking. They were sharing the burden of sadness as only people who are close can do. There was a lot to process. They both had deep feelings for this man, and yet they were strained feelings. His passing removed all expectations, and now they could look at what they liked about him and not what they hoped he would become. Ellen's Mom opened up more and recounted good times and fun things they did at the beginning of their relationship. Ellen could feel her love for her Dad. It made it easier for her to love him, too. Ellen couldn't remember the last time they talked about her Dad and really enjoyed the conversation. From street light to street light they talked, laughed, and wiped away tears, but it was so good. By the time they opened the door of their home again they were both tired and wanted to go to bed. They prayed together and went to their separate rooms. As Ellen lay there thinking she could hear her Mom crying. She had a very deep love for this man, and now he was gone. Often she was by herself, but now she was alone. Ellen's heart hurt greatly and only found relief when sleep overtook her grief.

Neither one thought to set an alarm and when they walked out of their respective rooms it was late. They did get dressed in time for the late service at church. They only told the closest of friends. They didn't want to try to explain how such a close relative could pass without them knowing. After service they drove home. As they walked passed the car they both stopped and looked at each other then back to the car. Mom reached into her purse and took out the key. With a push of a button the doors unlocked. She and Mom grabbed the two boxes that were in the back seat and went into the house. Once inside they set the boxes down in front of the couch and sat down. Mom wanted to pray, so they did, asking God to help them through this sad time and also thanking Him for meeting their needs. As they went through the first box they found his clothes and shoes and things like that. At the bottom were pictures. Not only photos of the family but pictures that Ellen had colored years ago and given to her Daddy. It made them cry. Some tears, at times, can be the reaction of pain, some, though, are tears of healing and relief. To find that this man who always seemed so mad and who treated them very poorly, really did love them in his own way. Like the visitor that brought the car had said, 'he always had a place in his life for both of them.' As they opened the smaller box they found mostly maps and owner's manuals and papers. There was one envelope that stuck out. It was newer and white, not all yellowed or old-looking. Mom looked at it, turned it over, then opened it. It was Dad's last check. It had not only two weeks' pay but also nine days of vacation and seven hours of overtime on it. They both sat stunned as they saw the amount, it was over three thousand dollars. Both were sitting there with their mouths open. They had no idea that he earned that kind of money. They saw the roll of money he would take out to pay for food or drinks when they were out, but this was beyond unbelievable. They almost always ate peanut butter sandwiches for several meals in a week and ran out of gas in the car, yet he was making a really good income.

Putting the negative thoughts a side, Ellen's Mom began to think what this money meant to them. The house was in desperate need of repair, and their old car needed some parts replaced and new tires. God had met all their needs. It was not only the money but that the money came through the man they loved and wished they would have known more. It was such a blessing to know it came from him, that he had provided it. Now they were excited at the possibilities. Ellen urged her Mom to take the new car for a drive. It didn't take much pushing before they found themselves tooling down the freeway. It was nice, very nice. It was only two years old and had low miles. It had all the bells and whistles; electric windows and locks, digital dash board, and the stereo was outrageous. They were both giddy, like kids at Christmas. They took turns driving all over town, singing with the radio, turning on the heat in the seats, opening the sunroof, and pushing all the buttons. They swung by the house, picked up the old car, and dropped it off at the repair shop. In the morning Mom would call them to let them know to fix the list and put on new tires. When they shut off the engine in front of the house it had been three hours. It had been so much fun. The day had been an emotional tornado, and now at day's end they were both done. They came in and sat on the couch. They agreed that the new week's demands were going to come early, so they went to bed.

The loss really didn't affect their day to day much. It had been just the two of them for such a long time. It did sadden Ellen that her Mom grieved so. Not that she shouldn't, but it was just that she missed him greatly most all her life and now she had to put it in perspective that he was gone. Strange how our hearts work. Ellen could only imagine that her Mom dreamed of a day when her wildly exciting knight in shining armor would come back to her, but now she had to face that it would never happen. In a few weeks she was much better, and the day to day busy schedule that they both had, helped them to move forward.

The needed house repairs were completed with the money that they found in her Dad's stuff and a group of men from church. Mom had mentioned to some of the women that she was blessed that the money came in for the repairs. One person talked to another, and the men in the church came over to see what needed to be done. As they made a list, so much more could be taken care of when Mom didn't have to pay for the labor. The money went to materials, and the men of the church gave two Saturdays to complete the tasks. Ellen and her Mom were blown away. These men, for free, came, with all their tools, and experience to fix floors, roof, toilets, doors, and move appliances. Many of the wives came with them to clean up the repair mess, fix lunch, and hand out drinks. There was sweat and strain, laughter and bantering. It felt like a family day of working together and having fun doing it. Ellen noticed how some of the husbands enjoyed working with their wives. How they would work as teams. If the ladies could help, they did; and the men were glad for the extra help. She recalled how Beth's Mom and Dad seemed to live and love each other, respecting each other, and each other's gifts and abilities. This was a relationship she desired her future to hold and started recording these qualities in her steps for life.

Mom was able, for the first time in a very long time, to put money in the bank in a savings account. She and Ellen knew the importance of a few dollars stored away, they had just never had the luxury of doing it. They still moved forward with the repairs and new tires for the old car. It was the car that Ellen drove, and she was happy as could be to have it. After the repairs she knew it would start all the time. It sounded so much better with the new muffler, and it didn't leave a puddle of oil everywhere she parked it. Water did still leak in when it rained, but with the new windshield wipers, she could now see the road in the rain. She embraced the thought that her Daddy did love her and took care of her. It made their relationship easier to accept. She still couldn't help but feel sorry for him. Why didn't he show the way he felt about them? Why wouldn't he want to spend more time with them and know who they really were? In the past several years his visits were less and less and shorter and shorter. He never gave her time to share with him her feelings, dreams, or plans. He never gave her the opportunity to hear his thoughts and experiences. Now he was gone. She would console herself with the thought that at least now he was free from running away, and hiding himself from them. She would never know what was an act or pretend with him, but she knew the love she felt from him when she was a little girl was too real to be anything but genuine, and that would be how she would remember him.

9

School, work, volleyball, church, the whirlwind schedule was crazy, but Ellen loved it. She was blessed with being organized, which helped keep the stress and worry to a minimum. She was excited about what God was doing in her life. She was seeing more and more how her steps of life were guiding her to do the things that she had felt, through prayer and talking to others, were important for a young lady who wanted to experience the most out of life. This made her feel more comfortable with who she was and confident in the abilities that God had given her. In all this planned chaos, she continued to have the desire for a relationship with the boy that God had chosen for her. She was surrounded by boys who wanted to be with her. Some were very nice, but none were the right one, she knew that. She was not going to settle or be distracted by someone God hadn't picked for her. She continued to pray for her, her Mom, and Beth in this personal area in their lives, and yet lived to enjoy life while she was waiting.

During the Christmas break from school, she tried to get more hours at work, and her boss was glad to oblige. She loved working around the holiday. The money was good and the atmosphere was often uplifting. Her boss was a believer in Jesus and ran the business as he felt God would want him too. Most of the workers weren't believers but they were great people and fun to be with. As always Ellen came into work early. On this particular morning she was called into the boss's office. She knew, as she made her way there, that he had hired a new person, and she would have to train them. Like before, it was no big deal, she enjoyed meeting new people. She hoped it was a girl from school. She had told several to apply, and maybe one of them moved on it. It would be fun getting to work with them. So with anticipation of meeting a new friend and facing a fun day of work, she bounced up the stairs and burst into the boss's office.

As the door flew open, Ellen tripped over the carpet and fell into the room. She did catch herself on a chair, but graceful, it was not. Her boss was surprised and jumped up to help her. Ellen started laughing at the silliness and in the embarrassment of it all. When the dust had settled she looked up at her boss who just smiled at his favorite worker and began to introduce her to the new employee. It wasn't one of her friends. It was some boy, which added to the embarrassment. She turned a bright red. Her boss said his name was Ray and then started in on his usual 'new guy' speech. Ellen didn't mean to be rude, but she had heard it so many times that it was hard to be interested in it. She kept trying to look at her boss as he spoke, but she found herself moving her eyes over to look at this new guy. Something was different about him. His eyes never strayed. He made eye contact with his new boss and every once in a while agreed with a 'yes sir'. Who was this guy?

When her boss was finished, the two of them walked out of the office and down the stairs. Now Ellen started in on her 'new guy' speech. It was much better than her boss's. At that point she kind of giggled, because she noticed that she and her boss both had standard, new guy speeches. Ray seemed a quick learner and caught on the first time given instructions. He was attentive and polite, and she would have to admit, kind of cute. At lunch time in the break room he easily took all the new guy kidding and grief that always happened. It was in fun and good natured. Ellen liked his smile and was looking forward to working with him in addition to everyone else. The day seemed to zip right by as they all worked together to keep up during this busy time of the year. As they were making their way to the time clock, the Boss asked if they would all plan on working ten hours the rest of the week. Most of them smiled, because they were there to make as much money as they could before school restarted. Also because the Boss would let them start early, and they could still do stuff in their evening hours of their Christmas break.

As the days flew by, the crew synced into a good routine. The work went fast, and they were able to produce more and more. Soon they didn't need to work tens any more. On that last Friday before they would all started back to school, the Boss was handing out checks. He then announced that since they all had done so well over the past two weeks, that he put a bonus in their checks. Ellen was overwhelmed when she found that her Boss had doubled her check. She went in to thank him, and he asked her to stay for a minute. He was a gentleman and didn't want people to talk poorly about either of them, so he walked her to her car instead of having her in his office alone. He told her that she was a natural for his company and wanted her to consider coming to work for him full time when she graduated. He explained that he knew her plan was to go to college. He wanted to tell her now so she could consider it against going away to college. He went on to offer that if she would work for him full time, he would pay for her college if she took night classes. It was a tremendous offer. She was overwhelmed. She thanked him, gave him a hug, and jumped in her car to go home and tell Mom.

Christmas break was over and school started up, so Ellen's focus turned back to her studies as planned. When she needed to work, she worked hard; and when she could play, she played hard. Volleyball season was outstanding. Her regiment of conditioning throughout the summer and fall along with the camps she went to paid off. The team did very well and made it to the playoffs. This time they advanced to the finals. Over the next two weeks there was a lot to keep straight and think about; school, playoffs, and work. That last one was the challenging one. The offer of starting full time after graduation was just a small part of the distraction. The main attention grabber was Ray. She knew she was growing in her feelings towards him, yet she wasn't sure if he felt the same way. He was nice to everyone and joked with the group. He never paid extra attention to her or tried to get her attention in any way. She tried to not let it bother her, so she kept concentrating on other things at hand. Trusting that God would make happen what was best for her. In the final round before state, the team was just out-matched, and their season was over. It was a great run and a new school record for wins in a single season. There was nothing to be disappointed in, but that couldn't stop the disappointment. Ellen knew that each experience, good or bad, was a teacher, and there were lessons to be learned. That isn't to say that it was easy not going all the way to State competition.

This did open up more time for her to study for the final quarter of the year. Her GPA was solid and she was pleased with it. She was comfortable with the curriculum in her classes and didn't think there would be any bumps in the road to graduation. That left Ray. What was up with that guy? She was bugged by boys often, but him? He just treated her as one of the team, nothing else. She was resolved not to push or make the first move. Determined that God would bring her the right man for her life, but she was getting a little anxious for something to happen.

One Saturday morning, she saw Ray and her boss talking. When they saw her coming they moved apart and acted kind of funny. It was an awkward situation when she walked up and said good morning. They both were being strange. She just thought that maybe she was being self-conscious, as always, so she went on doing her work. That day Ray and the Boss left about an hour early. Now she really thought that was strange.

When she pulled up in the driveway after work, Ray was sitting on the front porch. She smiled at him as she got out of the car. Walking up she could see he was nervous.

"What are you doing here" Ellen asked in an unintentionally shy manner.

"I need to explain some things. First, the Boss and I were talking about you this morning. You see, I, uh, wanted to ask you if I could spend some time away from work with you. My Dad taught me the right way to do that was to ask your Dad first. Well I didn't know where you lived, so I asked the Boss about this. He shared that I would have to ask your Mom. We left early to come over here, so he could introduce me, and I could ask."

Ellen was about to scream with excitement. She forced herself to stand still and let him talk, like she was calm and very mature. His nervousness made her like him even more. So many boys came off like they were doing you a favor to talk to you. Not Ray, his shyness made her feel very special.

He continued, "So I would like to see you sometime. If it would be ok, I could come over next Saturday night and we could spend the evening here? We only know each other from work, and I don't want you to feel uncomfortable, or pressured. Would that be ok?"

Ellen was surprised. No one had been so thoughtful when they had talked to her about spending time together. She didn't want to have to wait all week but didn't want to ruin what he had set up. "That would be fine," she said very calmly, then an idea hit her, so she continued, "but I'm not sure of my Mom's schedule, so next week may not work, but I do know she's off tonight." She looked down in embarrassment, from her boldness. Rats, she should've just not said anything.

Ray spoke up, and with something of a confident voice, asked if he could go home and get cleaned up and then come back in about two hours. He didn't want her to have to rush around getting ready or feel she had to feed him. Ellen agreed, walked up onto the porch, and closed the door behind her after saying 'see you in a little while.' Her Mom met her at the door, Ellen almost ran into her squealing.

"Wow he is so cute, and such manners, does he have an unmarried uncle or something?" Her Mom said. They both laughed as Ellen blushed. Her Mom was encouraging and excited for her that he was coming back. They made a plan on how it should work. Her Mom would be polite and sit and talk for a few minutes, then go to her room and read, coming out every 15 or 20 minutes to offer drinks and snacks and such. Ellen ran off to take a shower and get ready. She squealed again almost beside herself as she went, and Mom had to laugh, remembering the feeling.

Ray showed up right on time. She had just finished getting ready for him and was finding it a little hard to breath. They walked into the living room together, and her Mom said hello. Mom sounded so calm and confident. Ellen was hoping to sound that calm and gracious. Ellen noted again how much she admired her Mom. Ray sat on the couch at one end, allowing Ellen as much room as she wanted, so she sat in the middle. There was a little chit chat about school and family, then Mom went to read. They struggled a bit with what to talk about, then Ellen asked if he wanted to play a game or if he would rather watch some TV. To her delight he chose a game. That way, she thought, they could face each other and talk while they played. She wanted to look at him, especially in his eyes. She had learned a while back that you can learn a lot about a person by looking into their eyes, and his green eyes just invited a person to stare into them. The game was such a blast. They talked, laughed, Ellen made fun of how bad he was at the game, and he just agreed. Mom one time stopped to watch and had to laugh with them. Ray asked her to join them, and Ellen encouraged her to do so. The three of them played games the remainder of the evening and had a wonderful time. Somewhere around 11:00 Ray stated that he should head home. They all stood up. Mom mentioned how much she enjoyed herself, that it was nice meeting Ray, then made a quick exit. Ellen walked Ray to the door. She also said how much fun she had and how he was going to have to brush up on his game skills. They both laughed as he agreed.

"Can we do this again?" Ray asked.

"I would like that," she replied. "Do you have something in mind?"

"Well, I hope I'm not being too pushy but can I maybe come by and pick you up for church tomorrow? I'll just tell my parents that I'll be going with you."

"My Mom and I often go together."

Ray quickly jumped in and said they could all ride together. Then if they would let him, he would buy them lunch. He nearly begged. She asked him if he could arrive at 9:00, because they always went to Sunday school.

Ray smiled real big and replied, "Oh, that will be no problem, I planned on going to Sunday school too. So it's a plan; I'll be here at 9:00 and after worship the three of us will go out to eat, my treat." He waved, opened the door, and left. He never touched her.

She floated into her room to go to bed. His face, his words, but most of all his smile, helped her not to fall asleep for hours. When she did wake up, the anticipation of seeing him again in mere hours was invigorating. Mom just smiled when Ellen told her Ray was picking them up for service and said that she could drive herself, and the two of them could ride together. Ellen assured her it was Ray's idea and expressed concern that he may be disappointed if Mom didn't go with them, so she gave in and rode along. Ellen's Mom thought of how different her little girl was towards this boy than she had ever been. She wouldn't have ever wanted her parents around her and her boyfriends. She wanted to be alone with them. Mom was glad Ellen was different. She would likely make a better choice than she, herself, had. After all, Ellen was following God, which was something she had not done. After service the three of them went out to eat. It seemed that all three were a little apprehensive about how it would go, however the conversation quickly picked up and everyone felt comfortable. The lunch was, actually, a lot of fun. Ellen felt that Ray not only respected her Mom, but also enjoyed her company almost as much as Ellen did. This endeared him to her even more. When they arrived back at Ellen's home, she insisted that Ray come in and take another beating at the board game the three of them played the evening before. She noticed she didn't have to twist his arm too hard to get him to give in.

After Ray left in the late afternoon, Ellen asked her Mom if she would pray with her that she would know if he was the one she should be with. She didn't want to waste her time and risk her or Ray's heart on some kind of fling. She wanted it to be of God or not at all. They prayed that Ellen would know if this wasn't right, but if it was that she and Ray would be careful to handle themselves in a way that would be best for both of them and be right in God's eyes. The next day Ellen called Beth and set up that she would come by and talk to her after school. When she started sharing, the two of them reacted to each other's excitement like a match reacts to gasoline. They were both bouncing off the wall as details were shared and heard. When they finally did come back down to earth, Beth suggested that they pray about Ray and Ellen. When it was Ellen's turn to pray, she begged God that he would soon send someone very special for Beth. They both wanted godly men to make godly families.

On her way home, she stopped by Miss Sara's house. It was later in the evening, and the family had finished their meal. The kids were heading for bed, and Miss Sara's husband said he would finish getting children tucked in, so she and Ellen could talk. Much to Ellen's joy Miss Sara reacted like Mom and Beth. Each one of them encouraged her excitement. She was so happy and wanted to hear all the details. Miss Sara asked if he would be in church on Sunday and how they could 'accidently' bump into one another. After all the celebration and talking, Ellen asked Miss Sara to pray with her that this was God's will. As she was leaving, Miss Ellen's husband overwhelmed her by what he did. He came over and jokingly said that he didn't mean to eavesdrop but at their volume it was hard not to hear. He asked if he could pray with her with a daddy's heart. Tears quickly came to Ellen's eyes as she shook her head yes. This was a true godly man, striving to fill a need in her life.

Then he started, "Father, I stand here with Ellen to pray your blessing upon her. Father, having young daughters of my own I know what I hope for them, and I now pray these same blessings over Ellen. Please, Lord, give her wisdom at the very beginning of this relationship. If it is your will, confirm it, or if it is not ordained by you, please bring it to an end. I pray that this man, Ray, is a godly man who is also seeking your will in his life and that as both Ray and Ellen follow you, you will bless the desires of their hearts. May they bring You glory. Bless and protect their purity, and guard their hearts as they make these steps in their lives. In Jesus name, Amen.

Ellen hugged them both and drove home.

10

Continuing in her commitment to follow her 'steps for life' Ellen was once again reading over the things she had added in the past several weeks; remain focused on God as you enjoy life and others, finish well in all things possible, learn to build deeper relationships, memorize scripture, and so on. These were things the preacher would say during service or verses that impressed her in he Bible readings, even phrases spoken or sentences in a book, anything that she thought would help her be the person she wanted to be. This review kept things fresh in her mind and available to her. Often when choices would need to be made, she knew which one to take, it was like being prepared ahead of time. Some of the challenges she still had to consider longer, to weigh things out and look at pros and cons, but more and more, she had what she needed to make the best choice and to move forward with confidence. She found this helpful at work, at school, and in most all of her life. She felt that she was leaving mere common sense behind and starting to operate on Godly wisdom. It was becoming who she was which continued to encourage her in it.

She and Beth continued to spend quite a bit of time together. The school year was coming to a close, so they both would study together and keep an eye on the baby's needs. Ellen never minded taking care of the little JoE; she loved babies. Beth's grades had come up tremendously. She had started her own steps for life and was committed to living up to them. She and Ellen would often share the things they were using or adding. They encouraged one another, and even pushed one another. One of the things that was on Beth's list was to graduate. She was clearly on track to be able to scratch that one off the list. Being in the same Sunday school class now, doing their own Bible studies, and sharing the steps of life reinforced what they knew was true. It pointed them to the way they wanted to live and who they wanted to be. Beth knew that it was important, as she looked into the future, that she wouldn't think only of herself, she must think as a we not as a me. Ellen had told her that the ladies at church, especially Miss Sara, would be very helpful in words and example. They continued to pray with one another for their choices now and in the future. To say these girls were growing older and maturing into young ladies would almost be an understatement, unless you walked in on them when they thought the house was empty and their favorite song would come on. They would dance around and sing with the radio, using anything they could find as a pretend microphone; from hairbrushes and spoons, to their cell phones and soda bottles. They would have just good, crazy fun that was hilarious to the participants. It was a great relationship that these two shared. Different starting point, different choices, yet now walking the same road.

When Ellen was gone and Beth was home with the baby, it was harder to be positive and confident. She knew that she was missing fun stuff in school. She knew that nobody was thinking about her. She was positive that her life was just passing her by and was, for the most part, over. She would tell herself that Beth cared, and her parents loved her. She would remind herself that it was great to be a Mom, and she could feel the love that JoE had for her. However, talking to yourself and believing it are two different things. It was a constant battle. There were so many questions, big questions which constantly stared down at her. Many of which there were no answers to. Not now. It would take time, and life, and living; but that just seemed like a wall that was between who she was now and who she would be. A wall that she helped build. A wall that she couldn't tear down. It wasn't that she resented the baby, it was she couldn't get over how very stupid she had been. So careless with her life. Now what did the future hold for her and JoE? Only God knew, and it seemed He wasn't telling. She didn't want to be disrespectful to God, but her faith only carried her so far, then sorrow and fear would begin to creep in and start squeezing her. Prayer and pushing herself forward was the only way through, holding to the hope that God would bring roses from what she now saw as ashes.

Ellen and Ray continued to see each other. In small groups from church or work, or at each other's houses. It was so easy. They just enjoyed being together. They even spent hours over Beth's house. Ray connected with Beth's parents as easily as Ellen did. Beth loved making fun of Ray, and he would just smile and enjoy the fun right along with everyone else. He was somewhat quiet, but so comfortable with who he was that he could laugh with the good-hearted kidding. Most nights Beth and Ellen would feed off of one another and gang up on Ray. Sometimes Beth's Mom would tell them to stop and be nice. The girls would be laughing so hard they could hardly breathe. Ray just smiled and shook his head. It never bothered him. Ellen noticed how good he was with baby JoE. He would play with her and make her laugh. It was so cute to see them interact. It made Ellen's feelings for him grow.

One night when she and Ray had met separately over at Beth's house, she waited for Ray to leave, so she could talk to Beth's parents. She wanted to know their opinion of him. She started out by saying that she recognized that love can be blind, and because of that she wanted to know what they thought. She asked if they had any concerns about her relationship with Ray. This was one of the things on her steps for life, seek wise counsel.

They were glad to give their thoughts about Ray. They had talked between themselves previously about him and their relationship, and now they could be very supportive. They did mention that they had no conversation with him on many very important issues, but by what they could see, they thought he cared greatly for Ellen. They said it was obvious that he respected her and seemed to treat her well. They pointed out that they could see he was patient and tender with the baby and JoE liked him, which was a plus in his favor. From what they heard in conversation, it sounded like he was a guy with a plan. He had already chosen his college and had his classes picked out. They both thought planning and being organized was so helpful in any relationship and family. Beth's Dad talked about how he loved his sense of humor and the way that he took Beth's good natured kidding of him and laughed with everyone. Beth's Mom added that he clearly had a sweet and humble spirit. They were both very glad to see his relationship with Jesus was real and being lived out. Then they asked Ellen some questions.

"How is he around his Mom and Dad?" Beth's Dad asked.

"I have to admit, he is the same way over there as he is around here. He has the same quiet demeanor with a fun attitude. He is so nice and thoughtful to his Mom, and you can see he loves and looks up to his Dad. It so comfortable over there."

"Oh Ellen. that sounds great." Beth's Mom said. "How real does his relationship to Christ seem to you?"

"It seems as true as he is. When we have talked about the Bible and the things of God, he shows me things I've never thought of. The conversation is intriguing. I've never talked to anyone with his perspective and passion for the truth. I love it."

"Have you talked about where your relationship is going?" Beth's Dad asked.

"Ray has told me that he doesn't want to push me. He said that he has his ideas of what is next but would wait for me to ask him before he would share it. That is one of the reasons I wanted you both to give me your opinions."

"Well as we have said, to us, he seems to be a great guy, and we are very happy for you both. We know how much time in prayer you have invested in this, and we have been in prayer, too. So, what are you going to do now?" Beth's Mom asked.

"Well, we are supposed to grab a pizza after work tomorrow. I've about made up my mind to ask him where he thinks we are going in our relationship." In her cute teenage way, she gave a half smile, placed her arms in front of her, and clasped her hands together. Clearly she was nervous and shy about opening this subject. "It's getting late, and I still have things to do at home. I'd better go."

They all hugged and said their goodbyes. Ellen set up with Beth to call her later in the week. She walked out of the house and started to think about how she would ask Ray, and what the possible plans were that he had for them. With the shutting off of the car, she realized she was home and tired. She had decided to talk to Ray and committed to it in her head. She would wait to talk to her boss about his offer. She first wanted to find out if she should be thinking for herself or if it should be a she and Ray decision. She let out a little squeal and clapped her hands together quickly. With no real thought on her own, she knew it was ok to fall in love with him and she was almost overwhelmed by the thought. Some of it was relief, because she was sure the struggle of 'is this right' was over. The rest was pure love that filled her heart. When she got out of the car and started walking up the walk to their house, there sat Ray waiting again.

He smiled and stood up. They both knew the decision was made by God. It wasn't just them. For the first time since they had been hanging out, he walked up to her and took her in his arms. She had to tippy-toe to reach his neck; but as they held to each other, she was swept by security. They stood there hanging on to one another. When he finally let her go, she kind of laughed and said, "Wow! You sure know how to greet a girl." He turned red.

"When I left Beth's tonight, instead of driving home, I drove around. I was thinking and praying and trying to see what God had for us. I know I told you that I would wait for you to ask, but after tonight I have to ask if you're ready to ask me about our future."

He was bold and sure. He didn't stutter or look away. Now he waited for her answer.

"Ray, would you please share with me what you think the future is for our relationship." They both were saying what the other wanted to hear. It was no accident that the words used instilled respect and security along with excitement and anticipation.

"I'm very confident God is telling me that you should be my wife. I've talked to my parents and your Mom, along with the preacher and my Sunday School class. I've prayed a lot about this. We need to talk and see if God confirms this in you also. I would have waited till a better time, but I was about to explode." He stopped and waited.

Ellen was shocked that he went to that point. She had all the pieces of the puzzle, in the back of her mind somewhere she knew that would be the step, but she had never put it all together, let alone said it out loud. She had never, not even to Beth, said it out loud. Her head was spinning with the thought. Was he really proposing?

"Wait, I don't think that came out the way I hoped. Oh wow, I'm sorry. I'm not looking for that decision now. What I really meant to say was, I want to begin to go deeper into our relationship. Talk about what the future looks like for us, you and me, together. Oh I'm so sorry, I, I..."

"Wait," Ellen said. "On my drive over here I know God told me that it was ok to fall in love with you. Don't you see, our love for one another was confirmed at the same time? This is right and blessed, words are just words at times, but this is God moving in both our lives together at the same time. Yes, I want to talk about a future for us and what that means and all that goes with it." She smiled, tears rolling down her face. They hugged and then separated and looked into each other's eyes. Without hesitation Ray dropped down to one knee and began.

"Because God touched both our hearts and has confirmed through prayer and wise counsel, I would be disobedient if I don't ask you. Ellen, I love you and believe God is calling you to be my wife. Will you please make me the happiest man alive and tell me you will spend the rest of your life with me? Will you marry me?"

Tears were just rolling down her face. The scene was beautiful. Dusk had begun to come on, Ray on one knee, a slight breeze, there was no one else in the world but them. "Yes, yes, I will Ray. I will marry you."

He jumped up and hugged her. Right then applause broke out all over. Ray and Ellen were startled. From the front porch, Mom was clapping. On the sidewalk, strangers had stood. On the street cars, had stopped. All these people had waited for the answer and then hooped and hollered, clapped and celebrated. Ellen thought God could not have sent a clearer message of approval. She was overwhelmed. She ran and hugged her Mom.

"Are you happy for us?"

"I'm so happy, and proud. You deserve a good man, and I think God has sent him for you."

The crowd dispersed with shouts of celebration and congratulations. They both had school the next day and had to work. They confirmed their plans to talk after work tomorrow, then they hugged and separated. She wanted to talk to Mom more and then call Beth. He wanted to rush home and tell his parents. Maybe this is not the way it's done in the movies, but neither of them cared. They knew it was right, and they were in love. That's all that mattered.

With the morning Ellen was making a list of all the questions that she and Ray needed to answer and talk over. She still needed to catch the bus to save that gas money, but it was strange thinking about getting married and still going to school. Strange, but exciting and concerning. There were now even more things to think about and consider. Ellen had tried to make plans for the future. Her efforts to get scholarships, turned out to be dismal. Oh, she was awarded several for both academics and volleyball, but they couldn't be added together, and they didn't amount to much. It seemed to her that God was closing that door. She was leaning more and more toward accepting the position that the Boss had offered her. That way she not only would be earning a living, but she would also have her education paid for. Another advantage to that would be she really didn't have any leading as to what to study, and her boss said he wanted her to take business courses. It seemed that the answer had been given to her before the question had to be asked. Now she and Ray had so many things to talk about and plan for.

11

With all the anticipation it was hard to concentrate through the school day. Sometimes Ellen would be so excited she could have exploded, and her joy would build up to almost tears, then in the next instant her stomach would be in knots with nerves. What a roller coaster ride! She just kept trying not to think about it. Walking down the halls she didn't notice those around her. People would bump into her or talk to her, and she would respond, but her mind really wasn't there. It was like fast forwarding through a slow motion scene in a move, very strange. It was one of those days that you walk through, caught up in your own world. She made it from class to class and participated as best she could; but when she was sitting on the bus, waiting for it to leave the parking lot, she couldn't recall any details of the day. Now she was heading to work and would see Ray.

She walked in to the Boss's office to collect the paperwork for the evening. He didn't look different, the office was in the same messy disarray, he gave the same warm smile, the same kind words, and the usual instruction, but through her eyes and in her mind, nothing was the same. She and Ray both knew that the night's work had to be done first, so they jumped right into it. The crew was extremely funny and lighthearted, and Ellen couldn't quit laughing. As they passed each other they would high five or punch each other in the arm. By lunch the others on the crew were making fun of them, asking what was up. Ray and Ellen kept denying that anything was "up", trying to act as if nothing was different. The crew kept pushing and prodding more until it became the joke of the night. Ellen was loving it. She wanted to tell the world. She wanted to scream it from the roof top, but she knew they should talk first, so she waited, and the waiting just built the excitement. By the end of the shift all of them were dragging, all of them but Ray and Ellen, they both still felt like they were floating. They had worked hard and finished a little early, and now the last minutes were creeping by. Every time Ellen looked at the clock she swore to herself it hadn't moved; and as often as she looked she was probably right.

Finally they were done. The shift was over, and they were free. They had set up that, for the first time, they would be in the car alone with one another. Ellen had gotten off the bus at work, and Ray had driven his car. They were both starving, so they were heading to the pizza place. Ellen was wishing Ray's car had a seat that she could sit next to him, because that's where she really wanted to be. It came easy. They never ran out of stuff to talk about. It was comfortable to be together. There was no pressure to impress, no wondering about what the other was thinking, good or bad. The conversation jumped from school, to stuff at work, and then where to park in the pizza place lot and what table to sit at.

After they ordered and their drinks were brought out, Ray looked at Ellen kind of serious.

"Ellen, we have to talk about things, important things. There are a lot of things I really don't know about you or your opinion of. Can we talk about things like that?"

"I would like to. I kind of feel the same way."

Ellen stopped and waited so Ray could take the lead, and he did. "Do you think we will live around here or would you like to move somewhere?"

She felt good that he started and was glad it was we and not a you or me. "I've never thought about it much, and I'm sure there will be many things like that," she said."

"But to answer the question, for now, I think we should stay here. We have friends and family here. We also have our church and church family. It would seem to make more sense to start here and see if God opens a door or calls us somewhere else.

"Oh wait, I'm sorry, I want to pray before we go any farther. I should have done this before we started. Can I pray for us and this conversation?"

"Sure. I think we should. Go ahead." Ellen replied.

The pizza came out right then, so Ray prayed that God would bless them as they made plans and talked of future things. He also thanked God for putting them together and giving them a desire for one another and for Him. Then he thanked God for the food, and they started eating.

"I was thinking the same thing, for those reasons and a few others. Before I share I need you to know when I ask anything, I don't want you to tell me what you think I want to hear, I need you to say what you think. Then if we have to talk it out and compromise we will, but if we are not honest with each other we might miss God's will for our lives."

"That makes sense. Yes I will, thanks." Ellen liked him saying things like that, since it helped her know how to handle the situation. She wasn't scared, but she wasn't sure how to go about this.

"What do you think you will do with what the boss is offering you?" Ray spoke carefully. He wanted her input.

"Well, what I thought was, since he will pay for my school and let me work full time, that would be our best choice. What do you think?"

Ray smiled, "I'm with you, that's quite a deal he's offering you. You have really impressed him and proved to be a great asset to the business. He and I have talked about it. He's a good man and cares what happens to you. Ok, now we will need to find a place around here to live, since you will stay at work. I think I should stay at work part time and go to the Community College. With the scholarship I received for playing baseball, and the money I saved, we should have no problem with me only working part time. Does that sound right to you?"

"I think so, but won't that depend on how much the Boss offers you to work part time?" Ellen spoke kind of shyly. She was questioning what he said and that never went well when her Mom did that with her Dad. She studied his response, so she would know if she would ever do this again.

"That's a good point, and I'm glad you mentioned it. Here is what I did. I took how much we make now, that's why I asked you what you made an hour, because I don't think the boss will cut your pay. So if we stay the same in pay and you go to 40 hours, we should make this." Ray took a paper from his jacket and showed her his calculations, then he continued. "I called around and acquired some rental prices and subtracted that, and then we would have this much left over for food, utilities, insurance, savings, and stuff. Now this is just a rough outline budget. Of course we need to sit down together and bang one out, but this shows us that we could make it. It will be close but I'm confident we can do it."

She was relieved. He didn't get mad; he took his time. He didn't make fun of her; he made her feel helpful. This is what she wanted, a partnership, two people working together. Like the Bar's in her neighborhood and Beth's parents, she wanted to be like that, and she could tell he did, too.

"Ok now another question, I've seen you with baby JoE, what are your thoughts of a family? What does family look like in your mind, for us?"

"Well," Ellen started a little reluctantly, "This is what it looks like to me, kids, more than 3, maybe more than 4, we would leave that up to God." She felt comfortable to share what was in her heart. "I would stay home and raise the children, take care of you and our home, that's my dream."

"Perfect, that's what I was praying for. I would have never asked you to be a stay at home Mom, but that is what I wanted for my children. My commitment to that is to study hard and get a job that will support us. This may mean extra hours and other sacrifices for the first years, but I believe it will pay off after we invest.

"This is a harder one," Ray said, "We should know where each of us stands as far as money goes. I'll start, I have my college fund that my grandparents started for me when I was born. It's been added to through the years by them and parents and family for birthdays and things. I have put half of everything I've made in there. Now by the way it adds up with my scholarship we have enough for my two year degree. My car is not perfect, but it runs and is paid for. I also have $1,237.75 in my savings. Now it doesn't matter what you have or what you don't have, we just need to know where we stand."

"I want you to know that Mom and I worked to get by, so, I don't have much. I drive my Mom's old car. We may be able to buy it cheap. It's not great, but it does run. Besides that I have $445.50 in the bank." She looked down at the table, embarrassed.

"That's great," Ray said, "You don't have any debt, that's a huge plus, and you know how important it is to have a savings. Wow, that is really good, I think we're setting pretty well."

Ellen exhaled and relaxed. He just kept being so positive and encouraging. It made her feel even more confident that, not only were they making the right decision, but also that everything would work out. He presented that they would have to sacrifice and work at it and showed that they could do it.

"What about your wedding, our wedding? What will you want for it?" Ray asked.

"I'm not a big deal person. My Mom doesn't have the money. We can't spend the money. This is what I was thinking. See if your parents will let us use their back yard, and have the ceremony and reception there. My Mom and I could make some snacks and serve tea and lemonade. It's not the outside that matters to me, it's our hearts."

"Are you sure? This is the only wedding you'll ever have."

"Pretty sure of yourself aren't you?" she kicked him under the table, and they both laughed. She wished that they would have sat next to each other instead of across from one another. She longed to hug him and hold him close. She could see he felt the same way. She assured herself that he was just trying to respect her and not start a fire that they couldn't put out. She could clearly see in him the heat she felt. If it came together, it would be very hard to stop. Soon, there would be the right time and place for that. She looked forward to it.

They continue to talk about many things, most were much lighter. They finished their pizza and their sodas. When they got up to leave they saw, that not only were they the only ones in the place but that also the workers had completely cleaned up every area around them. She and Ray kept apologizing to the workers as they paid and walking out, but they were assured it was no problem. They sat down in the car and pulled out onto the street.

"Would you mind if I turn on the radio?" Ellen asked.

He would have let her do anything she asked, "Sure go ahead."

As the tunes came up Ellen heard one of her favorite songs. This was one that she and Beth used to sing to. Without hesitation she grabbed the volume knob and crank it up. Ray was surprised at how good she sounded! She had a pretty good voice, but the show was even better. Acting like she had a microphone in her hand, she sang very word. Bouncing in the seat to the rhythm, she never missed a note or the opportunity for an air guitar solo. He loved it. As they pulled up to her house, she just hollered, "Go around again," So he did. Three times around the block until the song and the one after that was over. It was the perfect encore to a wonderful first date. Ray met her at her car door and walked her up the sidewalk.

'Now he'll kiss me, I just know it, now he'll kiss me. I hope I don't have pizza breath…' . On her thoughts raced. They arrived at the door and faced each other.

"Ellen," Ray said, "I want you to be the only girl I've ever kissed, and I want that to be the kiss at our wedding. Do you think I'm dumb?"

Ellen just looked at him. Her head kind of tilted as she thought 'where did this guy come from.' Then, when what he had said sunk in, she said "No, not at all. No, that's not dumb at all, that's beautiful. You are one interesting guy." She punched him in the shoulder kind of hard and said, "See ya later, buddy." Then laughed and went into the house. She had a good right, and Ray rubbed his shoulder all the way back to the car. Ya gotta love her, he thought to himself.

12

So the weeks leading up to the wedding were full of questions and appointments to be kept. The invitations were nice and printed out on a friend's printer. The guest list was short, but people could invite others and bring their children. It was a casual affair. Ray was going to wear a suit that he had, and Ellen was going to borrow a dress from someone at church. Both their Sunday school classes volunteered to do the drinks and snacks, which was such a priceless gift and a tremendous blessing for them. Decorations came from Beth's parents whose backyard they were using for the wedding and reception. It would be a great setting. Questions came from several different directions but between Ellen, her Mom, Beth, and Ray the answers came pretty easy. Ellen continued to keep focused on the step of marriage and not get caught up in the stress and pressure of trying to making it the party of the century.

It was such a blessing how many people started volunteering to be a part of their day. Some of these people Ray and Ellen barely knew. One such person was the lady that told them, if they would let her, she would do the decorations in the back yard and the flowers for the ceremony. This was a mom that went to the church that they attended. Both had seen her before but neither of them had any more contact with her but to say hi now and again or wave. When asked why she would be willing to go through this work and expense for them, she replied that Ray had one time stopped and talked to her nine year old son. The conversation wasn't long or important, but it made an impression on her son. It was such an important example of how a kind hearted man lives his life. Any time when her son sees Ray, he still says, 'there's the guy that talked to me.' She went on to say that anytime she saw Ellen she was smiling and looked like she was enjoying life, and wanted to be a part of their wedding day. Some of the people in the praise band came to them and wanted to play music for the day. One of Ray's friends was in the band and had talked to the others. Others had offered to also help with food, or just asked if they could stop by. Ellen never realized that she knew so many people. At times it made her cry to think how God had worked in her life in such a wonderful way to give her so many people that wanted to be a part of their life on this day. Before long, they started being concerned about how many people would be showing up.

One day, Beth's parents came to Ray and Ellen and made a suggestion. It seemed obvious that their back yard was definitely not going to be large enough. Yet they knew it was the couple's desire to be married outside. Beth's Dad, who was a teacher at the High School, asked the School Board if they could rent the football field. When the Board found out for what, they agreed and made them pay a rental fee of $1.00.

"Now you can have the room you need," Beth's Dad said, "and everyone will have a good seat. We can use the bleachers."

Ray looked at Ellen and said, "Well you can hardly beat that."

"That's crazy," Ellen said with a smile on her face. "Now all we need is to get the marching band to attend." They all laughed.

They found out that this was going to be the first wedding out on the football field. Somebody called the newspaper and told them of the event. A reporter called Ellen and asked her a bunch of questions. Ellen was enjoying all the excitement the wedding was creating. The reporter then asked her who was invited. Jokingly she just said, "Well, I guess everybody. We have the room." Then she laughed. Two days later the article came out in the county paper. Ellen was giggling and enjoying the whole thing until she came to the part where the reporter put in the statement that the wedding was open to the public. Ellen's jaw dropped open. She really never meant that "everybody could come." What were they going to do? The phone started ringing off the hook. Everyone else thought the idea was, in their words, cute, funny, great, wonderful, and on and on.

Ray came by the house. To be honest, he couldn't keep from laughing. He just kept saying 'Well, you wanted a simple, small wedding'. Then he would throw in 'it couldn't of happened to a nicer girl.' Ellen was pretending to get aggravated. He slowed up a little when she punched him in the shoulder. She really did have a good right hook. Then they got down to work. They started by calling the lady that had graciously taken over organizing the food. They told her just to tell everyone not to fix anything. They would have the ceremony and leave. She was nice about it, but just flat out refused. They all had already ramped everything up, and if they ran out, well, who could blame them. Ellen was surprised at the way everyone just looked at the whole thing as a game, fun, exciting. The Mom that was doing decorations, enlisted her children and their friends to start helping her. Even the Dads were getting involve. Ray and Ellen didn't even know most of these people. Why would they all want to get involved in something that offered them nothing? Ellen thought it would make more sense if this really was a big deal put on by a big celebrity. But this was just a couple of nobodies. She wasn't even wearing a real wedding dress. It was just a white prom dress, used, for goodness sake. Ray would be wearing a suit. What were these people expecting?

Ellen turn to Ray and said, "This is kind of getting out of hand, don't you think."

He could tell she was getting worried. He hated to see her like that, and wanted to take care of her. "Ellen, nothing is really any different than when we were getting married in Beth's back yard. I really don't think that many people are going to show up to see some perfect strangers get married, and if they do, great! Maybe they will hear something that will spark some kind of interest in Jesus. There is no way they can come and expect anything from us but a seat in the bleachers. Don't let this get complicated when we can simply decide to keep it simple and let the chips fall where they may."

"Do you really think we can do that?"

"Sure," he replied. "Keep it light and fun. I think if we keep it easy and fun, anybody that would show up would catch that same feeling. How great would that be if, on our wedding day, we can make some strangers smile and enjoy their day? Do you agree?"

"Hey, you're pretty smart sometimes. But even a blind hog can find an acorn every once in a while." She laughed.

"Whoa, leave it to you to take a very sensitive, relational building moment, and turn it into a joke."

"A joke? Uh, no, I thought I was being completely encouraging." Ellen smiled, and punched him in the arm. Ray laughed and rubbed his shoulder.

The days whisked by. They became a blur as each detail was worked out. It seemed Ellen would roll out of bed and hit the floor running. With each step she worked at enjoying herself. Not being driven crazy by the questions and phone calls. At times she would just stop and take a half an hour or so to clear her mind, do some praying to keep perspective, and breath. Most days would end with her still having a smile on her face and looking forward to the next day. Her boss had given her a little leeway in her schedule so she had more time. Which she grabbed up and put to good use. Now the wedding was two days away and it was a 'ready or not here we come' kind of deal. Ellen and Ray said good bye at the Ellen's door. The Practice dinner was the next evening and then the big day. They were saying good bye and Ellen thought she would tease Ray a little. She moved as close to him as she could, then slowly moved her face to where they were almost touching, and in a low, soft whisper she said, "Ray please kiss me, I really would like you to kiss me." Then as he slowly tilted his head to one side, as she tiltied hers the opposite direction, Ellen jumped back and said, "oh no, we were going to wait for the wedding, right. Ewww, burn!" She laughed, punched him in the arm, and turned to go in the house. Ray knew he was going to bruise. He just smiled, shook his head from side to side, and walked back to his car as he could hear her laughing at her own joke. He loved her laugh. He would do almost anything just to hear that laugh.

They didn't see each other the day of the practice dinner. Ellen even had to call Ray and tell him that she would meet him at school by the bleachers. She just couldn't get finished at work in enough time to get home, get ready, and drive over to the school. She told him that she would just go over to Beth's, shower and borrow some clothes, then meet him there. Her Boss kept telling her to go, but Ellen would just say almost done, or one more thing. Finally he almost had to push her out the door. Ellen wasn't one to be late, but there was so much going on and needing to be done. Now out the door, it was a mad rush to Beth's. She called her on the way and told her the plan. Beth was her maid of honor and JoE was the flower girl being pulled in a wagon. Ellen parked in front of the house and ran up the walk, and only hitting about every third step, was in the house in a flash.

"Very elegant walk up those steps for a bride Missy," Beth's Mom remarked, and then they both laughed. Beth had the clothes laid out and the shower running. They were talking and giggling like they were back on the school bus the first day they met. A quick shower, comb through her hair, dressed and back out the door in record time. Last minute decorations in one arm, and the baby in the other, and the two girls were loading in the car. Mom yelled at them as they were jumping in, "Let Beth drive, she's not as wound up," the girls laughed and took the suggestion.

When they arrived at the football field they still had five minutes to spare. Most everyone was there and milling about. Ellen asked them to all gather around for a prayer. Ray and she had set it up previously that they would pray with the wedding party and parents before the practice. Without hesitation as soon as everyone was closer in Ray spoke up. "Let's have a word of prayer."

He spoke to God with such confidence. There was this tone in his voice that carried high respect for who he was talking to, but, at the same time, there was this familiarity that revealed a long relationship. The subject of the prayer was no surprise. The words used were clear but not overly impressive. But the conversation, and the comfort shown in that conversation, made Ellen cry. Her mind raced with thoughts, 'This is my Ray's voice. The man that wants to spend the rest of his life with me. Listen to him. He is going to be my husband.' The prayer was short but lasted for a million thoughts. 'Listen to the strength in his voice. Hear the compassion, confidence, and deep love for his God.' Ray's amen brought her out of her trance. She wiped her tears and acted like nothing had changed, but it had. Her love for Ray just grew to a height that she had never experienced before. It was now time for them to step through the service. Ellen strained to concentrate, for in reality all she wanted was to have Ray hold her. She wanted to hold this moment forever.

"Yes you walk in now, and then stand here. Ok start the second song. That right. Perfect?" On and on it went. They ran through it twice and it looked good. Most everyone was comfortable with what they were supposed to do and when, so they finished up there and all went to Ray's parents' house for the dinner. The evening was wonderful. Full of talk and laughter. Ellen was so glad that Ray's Mom and Dad and her Mom enjoyed each other's company so well. She had come to love his parents as much as Ray loved her Mom. Their friends got along great, too. There were some new people there that had come in for the wedding, Ray's grandparents and some aunts and uncles. Everyone was friendly and comfortable and joined in the celebration. Then it was time to go home and try to get some sleep. Tomorrow was the big day, and the butterflies in Ellen stomach already felt like fighter jets having a dog fight. She would be so glad when the wedding service was over and behind them. Many of the people that had remained were helping clean things up when Ray came up to her and told her to go on home and go to bed. He told her he would finish up the rest of the cleanup. She refused but couldn't lie to him when he asked if she was tired. Her day had started early and went late. She was beat. "Go on, let Beth take you home. Get some sleep."

She leaned into him, "This will be the last night we go home to separated beds." She pulled away, winked at him, blew a kiss, and walked away. Ray was wishing she would have just punched him in the arm. At least that stopped hurting after a while, that wink wouldn't leave his mind. He finished the work with a permanent smile on his face. He knew he really loved her. There was no question, and tomorrow she would be his for the rest of their lives. He would go to sleep as soon as he could stop thinking about her, and that wasn't going to happen any time soon.

Dawn came and found both of them in their separate houses kneeling by their separate beds, praying for each other. The perfect start to a perfect day. In time Ellen's Mom knocked on her door in a somewhat desperate manner. It was lightly raining and the forecast was for harder rain to come in by 3:00, the exact time for the wedding. Ellen's head exploded with thoughts. She jumped to the window and looked out. It was dark and gray. Small drops were hitting the window with frightening frequency. She was on the verge of tears. Then her phone buzzed. It was a text. She knew it would be Beth with the same concerns and wanting to think of plan B. To her surprise it was Ray. This is how it read. 'No worries, just believe and let the S-O-N shine and take care of everything.' So that's what she determined, God is able, and whatever He wanted to with the day was going to be ok with her. She didn't mind playing in the rain, and no matter the weather at the end of the day, she and Ray would be husband and wife. Nothing was going to stop that!

So the day went on as planned with no consideration of the weather what so ever. All the people that were helping were told that the celebration was on and to act as if it was a beautiful sunshiny day.

Shortly after 9:00 the rain stopped, and the decorations were checked out. No real loss, a few things had to be redone, but if the rain held off now they would be good to go. Ray called a Boy Scout troop that he helped with and asked if they would put on their full uniforms, come out around 2:00 and wipe off all the bleachers, then then stay for the wedding and line the walk way for the wedding party and the bride. Ellen had no idea. The young men thought it would be cool and all agreed, they even called another troop to help. There would be about 30 of them all together. Around noon big dark thunder heads rolled into the area. Thunder rolled and lighting jumped from cloud to cloud. Ray texted Ellen three words, "Hold the course.' She smiled and did. She was in the High School cafeteria for her final touches. The plan was that when it was time, she and the girls would walk out and get into her boss's custom van to be driven closer. Then, one at a time, they would walk about 30 feet down the sidewalk in front of the bleachers and then turn and walk about 20 feet down where the men would be standing. Each girl would meet her attending groomsman and walk with him another 10 steps, split and take their places in the line. Ellen would take her steps alone until she met Beth's Dad. He had always been a strong influence in her life. He was the Dad she never really had. When she asked him to give her away, he cried with honor, and here he was again standing, waiting to walk her to her beloved, with tears already rolling down his face.

In all the excitement and preparation of the day Ellen had totally forgotten about the invitation that was in the paper. The van pulled up in such an angle, it was impossible for the girls to see the people sitting in the bleachers. The thunder they could hear in the distance was a constant reminder of the threat of rain. Then the music started, just like they practiced. The door of the van opened, and the first girl stepped out. Her eyes widened with surprise, and she quickly glanced into the van and then moved away. Ellen thought to herself that it was strange, but maybe it was just a last look at the bride. Ellen was so excited. The next girl stepped out and jumped a little as if startled, then giggled and moved away. Now it was just Beth and Ellen. "Don't say anything, or I'll cry all the way to the altar." Beth just gave her a kiss and was gone. Ellen wiped Beth's tears from her cheek and moved to get out. The prom dress was easy to move in and Ellen was glad. The procession music stopped, and Here Comes the Bride started. Ellen stepped from the van as eloquently as she could and then looked up. She froze. There in front of her lining the side walk were 30 Boy Scouts in their uniforms, jumping from at ease to attention, and holding their salute. But the real shock came when the people in the bleachers stood for the bride's entrance. There must have been 500 people in the stands. She had never, not at any sporting event, ever seen so many people in those seats. Her face must have shown how stunned she was for many of the people laughed. Ellen knew she was as red as a stop sign, and her embarrassment made her giggle. Unconsciously she covered her mouth with her hand. The crowd loved it. She moved on. Those 30 feet looked like a mile. Striving to step with the music she passed the first Boy Scout. He snapped his salute. Ellen jumped sideways. The crowd was enjoying every minute with her. Not laughing at her but with her. Even the Boy Scouts who were trying so hard to be military had to smile. She recovered with grace and a smile and continued down the walk. She couldn't help but notice the change when the sun came breaking out.

At the appropriate place she turned left to go and meet her groom. About half way down was Beth's Dad, cheeks wet with tears, but with a smile of encouragement. When she finally reached him, he held out his arm to her. As many times before, she not only took it, but leaned on him, allowing him to lead her the remaining steps to Ray. She was beautiful. Ray was captivated. The sun made her hair shine, the breeze moved her gown to make it seem as if she was floating, but her eyes held his gaze. They say that the eyes are the window to the soul. If that is true all Ray could see was love. He was overwhelmed. She moved to his side allowing him now to not only see his beloved, but also to catch the softest hint of her perfume. The Preacher said something about 'who gives this woman to me married?' After Beth's Father shook his hand he took Ray's hand and placed Beth's hand in it. Her hand was so soft he almost couldn't feel it. 'Do you take this man…, Do you take this woman…, step by step, it wasn't that he was being disrespectful to the service, but he was just so overwhelmed that this day, this time, had finally arrived.

They gave a rose to the parents. Ellen's Mom kissed his check and whispered, I'm so happy to call you Son. Then when his Dad hugged him he quickly spoke in his ear, "God has really blessed you. Cherish her." They came back and stood facing each other. The preacher prayed over them, and asked God to bless them. Then speaking in what seemed slow motion the preacher spoke the words that Ray had been waiting to hear, 'You may kiss your bride.'. For the very first time Ray and Ellen's lips met to seal the commitment they just made to one another. The crowd literally went crazy. The roar was almost deafening. They both laughed, which ended the kiss, and turned to walked toward the jam-packed bleachers. The yells, whistles, and applause just increased. Before they turned to walk to the van, they stopped. Ellen graciously curtsied, and Ray bowed. It was a respectful gesture of appreciation. The people applauded even more. They understood what the newly married coupled offered to them, a heartfelt thank you for sharing their day with them. They then stood up, grabbed each other's hand and ran for the van.

www.ingramcontent.com/pod-product-compliance
Lightning Source LLC
Chambersburg PA
CBHW070450170726
48291CB00005B/1683

* 9 7 8 1 9 4 9 7 4 6 4 4 0 *